X          Japan          1.95 $\mathbb{C}^{m}$

# A BADGE
# AND A GUN

### by

## VINCE DESTRY

"Get me *El Diablo* or be hanged," the governor told Reed Loder. It was really no choice at all; Loder's back was to the wall. So, with every hand against him except that of one old town tamer turned town drunk, he took to the badlands to earn his right to a new deal through gunsmoke.

# A BADGE AND A GUN

# A BADGE
# AND A GUN

by

*VINCE DESTRY*

*LENOX HILL PRESS*
*NEW YORK*

*First published in the U.S.A.
by Lenox Hill Press 1975*


*Published in Great Britain
by Robert Hale and Company*

*©Copyright 1970, by V.G.C. norwood*

*2*

**Library of Congress Cataloging in Publication Data**

Norwood, Victor George Charles.
  A badge and a gun.

  I. Title.
PZ4.N865Bad3   [PR60064.079]   823'.9'14   75-2123
ISBN 0-517-52165-2


*Printed in the United States of America*

# A BADGE AND A GUN

# CHAPTER ONE

It was a little after midday. The back-country "howler" had blown since daybreak, a regular "twister," stirring the dust into whirling clouds and blotting out much of the daylight. Along the ridge, tall trees bent in the wind, threshing violently. Beyond, the bleak background was dim, hazy, a broken terrain stretching as far as the eye could see into the distance. To the west rose the southernmost extremity of the Rockies, fringing the badlands that extended clear to the Grande. To the southeast lay the great plains.

Through the cottonwoods a rider appeared, heading his mount from the partly protecting brush into the open and curbing the animal's snorting efforts to turn aside with an iron grip on the reins. Even hunched as he was in the saddle, the man's height was apparent, his breadth of shoulders tremendous. His hair, worn long, was black as a raven's wing, sweeping the base of his thick neck. His flat-crowned hat was thonged down, the brim fluttering. A green neckerchief protected his nose and mouth from flying grit. He wore a buckskin coat over a faded blue shirt and black levis tucked into scuffed knee-length boots. The butt of a six-gun holstered low against his lean flank bulged the coat out.

A big man, Reed Loder, rangy, all muscle, bone and solid flesh, pared to hard leanness by long hours in the saddle. His hands, large and long-fingered, bore no rope calluses, nor were they thickened through toil. Above the bandana his eyes, closed to mere slits, peered toward the vague outline of sprawling buildings huddled in a timbered hollow far below.

"Trail, Satan, damn your ornery hide!" he muttered. "I reckon that's San Rosa yonder. We'll rest up a spell and get something to eat. Mebbe by mornin' this dad-blamed storm will have blown itself out."

The big black's immediate response was to turn its head quickly and try to take a lump out of the man's leg. Loder countered the sly move with a firm rein and a strong wrist, and held the stallion into the gusting wind.

The town, when they reached it, was quiet, the streets deserted. Huge balls of tumbleweed bowled along the rutted main drag. Wind moaned under the eaves and clattered rusty iron sheeting. A lot of the windows were shuttered, doors closed. Here and there a horse stood dejectedly, hitched to a rail, head drooping, scuffing the dust with impatient hoofs.

Loder reined in outside a squat building and squinted at the creaking sign. "Badger's Rest," he read. He dismounted, looped the reins over the warped rail and clumped up the low steps. A square of canvas was draped beyond the batwing doors to help keep out the swirling grit. Loder pushed past and paused just inside, slapping dust from his clothing with his hat. He unfastened his coat and thrust the buckskin back, away from his holster. The leather was black with oil and worn smooth, polished with use and trimmed away to facilitate an easy draw. The gun was a Colt forty-four, its grips of carved bone, yellowed with age and constant handling. A gunfighter's weapon, and lethal, holstered at a level so that Loder's hand brushed against the butt as he walked.

Standing, he topped six feet by several inches. His face had a ruggedness, as if carved from stone. He wasn't a handsome man, but there was character in every line of his weathered features. His eyes were bleak. Men, recognizing the brand of the gunslammer on him, scowled and edged away from the long bar as his chill stare swept the crowded room. Loder replaced his hat, approached the counter and nodded to the fat barkeep. He ordered whisky, adroitly trapped the bottle the bartender slid across the scarred wood and reached for the glass that followed. He poured, maintaining his grip on the bottle.

"Leave the bottle," he said. "It'll take more than one to cut the dust outta my throat, mister."

"Bad blow," the man said nervously. "Worst snorter to hit these parts in a coon's age. Don't recall seein' you around here before, stranger. Just passin' through?"

"I reckon, if it's any business of yours."

"No offense, mister. Just makin' conversation is all. Will you be wantin' a room?"

Loder nodded. He tossed a gold piece on the bar.

"Best take it for now," he said. "I'll likely be leaving early, before anybody's about."

The bartender picked up the coins. In one corner, five men grouped round a table were conversing in low whispers. Loder heard his name mentioned. A thin smile twisted his lips. In the large mirror above the bar he watched the men, saw significant nods and jerks of the head.

"You got a barn round back?" he asked. "I'll be wanting a stall and feed for my hoss."

The barkeep nodded.

"Sure," he said. "That'll be a dollar extra, Mister Loder. I reckon you are Reed Loder, ain't you?"

"I'm Loder. So what?"

"Nothin'," the man answered quickly. "I saw your

12

picture in the *Waco Gazette* a piece back. I reckon 'most everybody in Mesa County's heard of you."

Loder drained his glass and poured another drink. He frowned. Ever since that damned newspaper had splashed his likeness all over the front page his name had been on everybody's lips. Reed Loder, a gunfighter, an ex-Ranger, turned sour, so men said, over a woman. The fastest man with a gun in the whole country, some claimed, despite the fact that two years ago, while he was still riding for the law, renegade lead had broken his right arm below the elbow. The wound had healed clean, and there was no damage to the bones. The stiffness had passed. For a time the injury had slowed his phenomenal draw. But with constant practice the muscles of his forearm eventually regained their suppleness.

Even so, the incident had aroused speculation. Reed Loder was not the hellion he used to be, some men said. Other hombres maintained he was as fast as ever, and a whole lot meaner. Since the shooting, Loder had been obliged to prove his gun swiftness many times, and there were lonely graves along his back-trail as somber evidence of his prowess. Whether or not he was still the best was something no man could determine until the supreme test left the issue in no doubt. Certainly, no man had ever pulled a gun on Reed Loder and lived to brag about it.

# A BADGE AND A GUN

His evil reputation was known from Abilene to
Laredo. As a Ranger he had made many enemies, and
since turning in his badge he had made a lot more.
Now he lived by the gun, a drifter, a man alone,
without prospects or any real hope for the future. A
hard, embittered hombre, only Loder knew the real
reason why he had cut loose from the Rangers and
taken to the dim trails. For a while after Molly Bergen
died, he had gone to pieces, started drinking heavily.
Liquor and the law didn't mix. Through an error on
Loder's part, a young lawman had died, cut down in
an outlaw gun trap. Had Reed Loder been sober at the
time, he could have warned Keith Moran, for a
Mexican kid whom Loder had befriended had brought
him word of Jud Chisholm's intended raid on the
Ratten City bank.

But Loder, brooding and morose, had been too
drunk to grasp the significance of the message, and
when he finally realized what was happening, it was
too late. It was the weight of Keith Moran's death on
his conscience that prompted Loder to quit the
Rangers, and it was whisky that inflamed his grief-
soured disposition until he shot and killed Frayne
Walcott on Reonada's main street. Walcott had been
notorious as a gunslinging trouble-maker, and his
death provoked a series of incidents until, without the
backing of a law badge, Reed Loder became just

another drifting gunhawk, forced to kill again and again or fill a Boothill grave.

He salved his conscience with whisky. No man would give him an honest job, but there were plenty who had need of his gun and who were willing to pay for his services. And after a time it didn't seem to matter any more what he did or how he lived. Though not much more than thirty, he looked forty. Already there were streaks of grey among the dark hair along his temples. He had no roots, no plans. Just staying alive was chore enough. And for the past few months the law had taken an interest in his activities. When he gunned Trull Mannion, friends of the dead man had claimed it was murder, and they had raised a stink that had eventually reached the governor himself.

There had been other shootings, too, concerning which the law had not been satisfied, though few lawmen in the territory had sand enough to arrest Reed Loder, whatever their personal convictions. But of late there had been other protests, and eventually the newspapers came out with a vicious attack on Loder and men of his ornery breed. His years as a lawman were skipped over. Emphasis was given to what he had become, to the men he had killed. The *Waco Gazette* had called him a murderer. Some fool, a friend of Trull Mannion, harangued politically influential friends to campaign for a clean-up in the state.

Reed Loder bore the brunt of it all. Officially branded an outlaw in some parts of Texas, and with a reward of five hundred dollars offered by the Mannion faction for his apprehension, dead or alive, he became the target for bounty hunters as well as swaggering gunslammers eager to prove their skill with a six-gun, and salty lawmen keen to gain a reputation by bringing in Reed Loder. He was not alone. Pressure had been brought to bear on the governor, and with election close, Kendrick couldn't afford to antagonize Mannion's friends. He issued orders calculated to drive rustlers and gunfighters out of the territory, gave circuit judges and town marshals extra powers in an attempt to stamp out increasing lawlessness.

But there were those who did not scare and who would not run, men such as John Wesley Hardin, Linus Conroy, Dobe Selbourne, and the sinister border raider, *El Diablo*, whose ragged wild bunch had raised hell along the Rio Grande for the past four years, robbing gold shipments, rustling, ravaging the vast trail herds pushing southwest, keeping settlers out, and dominating the whole area. An army could hide in the arid badlands south of El Paso and northwest, towards Silver City. The whole territory was infested with outlaws, but few of them created such extreme problems as *El Diablo*, a mysterious, almost legendary figure few men had ever seen, but whose name was spoken in whispers all along the border. *El Diablo*—The Devil. He rode down from the hills with his evil crew, robbing and burning, raping, murdering anybody who resisted, appearing suddenly, never twice in the same place. They struck, then vanished like phantoms into the badlands. Even a reward of five thousand dollars had failed to lure *El Diablo* into a bushwhack trap, and no law posse had been able to flush him from his hide-out.

Men had tried to earn the bounty and died with their boots on. Many a lawman, striving to penetrate those grim badlands fastnesses, had ridden into an ambush and had left his carcass for the buzzards. The Rangers, based in Laredo, were short of men and fully occupied with large-scale rustling and gangs of outlaws operating out of Waco and Dallas. With the threat of war again imminent, and Zachary Taylor campaigning to avenge the Alamo against Santa Ana, the Rangers were committed to ride with the Second Dragoons and couldn't spare men for civil duties as far northwest as Mesa County. Matters were coming to a head, the whole of Southern Texas uniting in the continuation of the fight against Mexico. Governor Kendrick had his problems, but they were of local importance only. He could expect no official help for some time. Meanwhile the reign of lawlessness continued.

Reed Loder, busy with brooding thoughts, poured again. He peered into the liquor, studying its amber clarity. He felt weary. The whisky was having a soporific effect, and he could hardly keep his eyes open. Idly he fingered the front of his coat, felt paper crackle in his inside pocket and remembered the letter. Thinking about the contents, he wondered again at the unexpected turn of events that had brought him to San Rosa, headed for the badlands and the town of Twin Rivers. His fingers, moving upward, encountered a hard metal object and pressed it through the buckskin, tracing its shape. A grim smile formed on his lips. The letter bore the signature of Jason Kendrick, governor of the state. It summoned Loder to a personal interview, offered him a chance to wipe out his past and make a fresh start. But there were conditions . . . .

"You want I should tend to your horse, Mr. Loder?" the bartender asked, breaking in on the gunfighter's musing.

"Reckon not, friend," Loder answered. "I'll see to the critter myself. He's liable to chaw your arm off. Can you rustle up something to eat?"

"You name it, mister."

"*Bueno*! Steak, rare, with fried potatoes and

onions, and a wedge of apple pie to follow. Plenty of sweet coffee. I'll take it in my room after I bed down my hoss."

The barkeep nodded. Loder raised the glass to his lips, but lowered it again when the rear door opened noisily and wind gusted into the long room, swirling grit and dust across the floor. A tall, stoop-shouldered man pushed past the drab drapes that concealed the approach from the rear of the building and slouched round the end of the counter. He had a thin, wolfish face and shifty, deep-sunk eyes.

"Give me a snort," he ordered. "Don't show any sign of lettin' up outside. I reckon it's—"

He broke off. His gaunt body stiffened. Reed Loder, glancing up at the big mirror, studied the newcomer's reflection and swore when he recognized the man. Brice Ruskin, a former deputy sheriff turned bounty hunter, an unscrupulous, ornery hombre, as mean and treacherous as a sidewinder and as deadly. Obviously the bartender didn't know who Ruskin was. The man was unshaven. His clothing was crumpled and travel-stained. A Colt forty-five with black wooden grips weighted down a cut-away holster thonged low against his lean left thigh. The butt of the weapon faced forward, although Ruskin was normally right-handed. A long-bladed knife was sheathed well back along his broad, plain belt. Long hair, dirty grey in color, swept the shoulders of the black leather coat he wore over a green shirt and calfskin vest.

He turned quickly, his head jerking round, and Reed Loder, realizing that Ruskin had recognized him, put down the brimming glass and leaned on the bar. He had tangled with Ruskin a couple of times in the past. The bounty hunter still carried Loder's lead in his fleshy shoulder. Twice Ruskin had tried to gun Loder from ambush. Neither time had Loder actually seen the man, and he had no positive proof that Ruskin had been the hombre who had tried to kill him. The only evidence was blood splashes and a spent cartridge case, and footprints. But Ruskin had bragged, when drunk, of how he had come close to nailing Reed Loder's hide, and word had reached Loder.

He hadn't bothered to look for Ruskin, figuring that sooner or later the man would try again. Now Ruskin's expression betrayed his surprise at seeing Loder. Obviously, if he had been trailing the gunfighter, he hadn't expected to catch up so soon. The bounty hunter was touch and vicious, fast and accurate with a gun or a knife and handy with his fists, though not a man to take chances—unless he thought he had the edge.

Ruskin stood scowling, staring at Loder. His right arm was across his body, the fingers of his right hand clawed above his holster. Abruptly he drew the weapon, eared the hammer back, then took a few swift steps toward Loder. Men, quick to recognize impending trouble, moved hastily away from the bar. The hum of conversation quieted.

"That'll be far enough, Ruskin," Loder said quietly. He made no attempt to reach for his gun. A contemptuous smile curled his lips. Ruskin halted. He licked his lips.

"Don't try anything, Loder," he rasped. "I've got the drop. It's been a long time, gunslinger."

He grinned wolfishly. Only the drag of his thumb held the six-gun's hammer spur.

"I allowed I'd catch up with you sooner or later," he mouthed. "Didn't hardly reckon it would be this soon. I've gotten a paper, Loder, empowerin' me to arrest you—for murder. Resist, and I'll kill you."

Loder regarded him bleakly. The place was suddenly very quiet.

"I always figured it was you I put my brand on a while back," Loder said. "Never thought you'd be fool enough to show your hand this way. A week ago I'd have gunned you on sight, you bounty-hunting buzzard. But now things are kind of different, so I'll pretend I didn't hear your brag and let you walk out of here."

Ruskin licked his lips again. He sneered. Something

he knew, or thought he knew, gave him more confidence than usual.

"You tell it scary, big man," he gritted. "Mebbe there was a time, a while back, when I'd have eaten crow rather than buck you, Loder. But not any more. I heard about Corey Nash bustin' your gun arm. They say that's why you quit the Rangers, Loder. I only heard about it recently. I reckon that just about cuts you down to my size, hard hombre. Somebody finally de-horned the great Reed Loder. Wal, I've ridden a long ways to collect that five-hundred-dollar reward they're offerin' for your scalp. I aim to take you in, Loder. Shuck that gunbelt, slow and easy."

Reed Loder sighed. He stepped away from the bar, turned slowly to face Ruskin and carefully opened his coat. He held it open. Sunlight, filtering through the grimy windows, gleamed on metal—a five-pointed star pinned to the breast pocket of his shirt.

Seeing the badge, the bartender's eyes widened. He sucked in his breath sharply, swore with surprise. An excitable muttering circulated among the gathering. Men stared, gaping blankly. Ruskin's lower jaw sagged.

"Them reward posters are ancient history, Ruskin," Loder said harshly. "I'm riding for the law ag'in. Best forget the five hundred and put that gun away."

Ruskin's eyes narrowed. The badge was that of a

# A BADGE AND A GUN

U.S. marshal. Ruskin swore.

"What is this?" he demanded. "You ain't no peace officer, Loder. Why, you two-bit gunslinger, what kind of a rusty are you tryin' to pull? I'm warnin' you, Loder. Whatever it is, it won't do you no good. I dunno how you came by that star, but I'm takin' you in, badge or no badge, and let the sheriff at—"

Reed Loder's right hand blurred. Not a man in the room actually saw him draw. But suddenly the room was filled with acrid powdersmoke, and Brice Ruskin was staggering back, gripping his right forearm. His gun thudded onto the boards. Blood from a deep bullet groove across his flesh spurted through the lead-torn sleeve of his coat. Face ashen, he stumbled against the bar.

"I should have killed you," Loder told him. "I never did cotton to sneakin' bounty hunters, Ruskin. It don't always pay to believe all you hear. This badge means what it says—U.S. marshal. You can forget the dodgers. Be out of town by morning, or I'll see to it that you rot in jail for the next six months. You got a lawman in this town, bartender?"

"Ben Riggs is town marshal, mister. But he's out around Gopher right now. Won't be back much before noon tomorrow, I reckon."

Loder nodded.

"That's a break for you," he told Ruskin. "Now git!

23

Next time I'll do more than crease your arm. Leave the gun.''

Cursing, Ruskin lurched toward the main entry, angrily wrenched the tarpaulin aside and shoved out into the street amid clouding dust. Reed Loder punched the spent shell from his gun, replaced it with a live round, then leathered the weapon deftly.

"In case any of you hombres are wondering about this badge," he said, "it was pinned on where you see it by Governor Kendrick himself. I reckon you couldn't have it any more legal than that. I ain't minded to answer a lot of damn fool questions, but I'll tell you this. I'm riding southwest to do a job, and you can pass the word that Reed Loder's riding for the law ag'in and aiming to smoke out the thieving skunk who calls himself *El Diablo*.

Another ripple of excitement spread through the room. Loder turned to the barkeep.

"I'll tend to my hoss, bartender," he said. "Then I'll have that chow up in my room, soon as it's ready. You got a washroom upstairs?"

"First door on the left, mister—er, Marshal. Can't rightly get over that badge. Sure came as a powerful surprise. Why, it ain't hardly a week since I read in the *Gazette* about you bein' a wanted man, and—"

He checked his outburst when he saw the anger clouding Loder's expression.

"I'll fix the grub," he said lamely. Loder nodded. He strode toward the rear doorway and went out, creating a draught. With neckerchief drawn up to cover his mouth and nostrils, he moved along the gloomy back street and approached the livery stable on the corner, leaning into the tearing wind, hat tugged low, brim fluttering. As he stepped off the narrow boardwalk into the rutted drag, gun flame stabbed the haze from across the street.

A bullet plucked at the buckskin between his left arm and his ribs. The report came, cracking spitefully—the loud, whiplash reverberation from a Springfield rifle. Loder whirled, crouching, his six-gun already drawn and bucking against his palm. He shot toward the gun flash, thumbed the hammer spur twice and heard the unseen assassin scream hoarsely. A tall figure sagged out from a murky opening and pitched headlong. The man flopped over, then lay still.

Loder approached warily, shielding his face and eyes from flying grit. He flopped the corpse over with the toe of his boot. The dead man was Brice Ruskin. The bounty hunter had been shot through the chest, and his injured arm had been broken above the elbow. The first slug, ripping through his heart, had killed him instantly. Loder, grim-faced, reloaded automatically and holstered the weapon angrily. He had thought the sight of the badge might deter Ruskin after the incident in the saloon.

He went round to the front of the building, unhitched the big black horse standing with its hind quarters to the wind and led the animal to the side. The barn door was closed and tightly secured, and with the wind blowing full against it, Loder had a struggle to get it open. He held the heavy planks wide until Satan was inside, then let the door bang shut. The latch dropped on the outside, fastening him in. There was no sign of the hostler. Sufficient daylight infiltrated to enable Loder to see what he was doing. He put the horse in a stall, unsaddled him and provided ample oats and hay, then left by a small side door.

Back in the saloon, he gave the bartender a dollar.

"That's for the hostler, when you see him," he explained.

"We heard shootin'," the man said, nodding absently.

"Ruskin tried to drygulch me in the alley. I had to kill him. If the marshal gets back before I leave in the morning, if he wants to see me I'll be in my room. You can bring the chow any time it suits you."

Loder finished his drink, then approached the staircase and mounted the treads slowly. Behind him, a tumult of raucous conversation and argument developed. Oblivious to it, Loder dumped his saddle in

26

the room allocated to him, located the washroom, and was back in the room when the bartender brought the laden tray. Later, with hot food in his belly, Loder sprawled on the creaking bed, fully clothed, and smoked. Despite mental and physical weariness, his mind was too heavily burdened for sleep to come immediately. He thought back to his talk with Governor Kendrick. No man could have been more surprised than Loder when he got Kendrick's letter inviting him to meet the man, for only a couple of months before, the governor had signed documents putting a price on Loder's head for the alleged murder of Trull Mannion.

He had obeyed the summons only after considerable deliberation, suspecting some sort of a trick at first, remembering how the law had connived in the murder of Jesse James and the shooting of Billy the Kid. But Jason Kendrick had a reputation for being straight, and eventually Loder had taken a chance. He rode into Austin at night, prepared to shoot his way out. But there had been no trap. Governor Kendrick was as direct in his speech as he was in doing state business, the gunfighter soon learned. With a drink by his elbow and a cigar in his mouth, Loder, seated in a comfortable armchair, had listened.

"I asked you here to talk plain and straight," Kendrick had told him. "I won't beat about the bush,

Loder. I'm determined to stamp out lawlessness in this part of the country. The day of the gunslinger is passing. Once this conflict with Santa Ana is determined, the country will open up, start to grow and develop. There's no room any more for your kind, Loder. Your father was a good friend of mine. That's one reason I'm giving you this chance now. If you're smart, you'll take it."

"Knowing my dad didn't prevent you from putting a price on my head, Kendrick. I didn't murder that fat louse, Mannion. It was self-defense."

"Seems to me I've heard that before, too, Loder. I had to go on the facts as supplied by the sheriff of Tecumseh County. But I didn't bring you all these miles to discuss that. Apart from Mannion, whatever the circumstances, you've shot to death more than twenty men. Hardly a recommendation for good conduct. I always liked and admired your father. He was the best lawman Texas ever raised. But you—well, you've been going steadily downhill ever since you quit the Rangers. Nobody blamed you for young Moran's death. You'd had a shock, a bad body blow. Reasonable men make allowances for grief, Loder. You should have stayed. But I won't go into that. There can be only two endings to the trail you're following. You'll either wind up in a Boothill grave or at the end of a rope. Even discounting Mannion, there's grounds for sending you to the penitentiary at Yuma for many years, on the evidence in hand."

"Evidence? The vicious testimony of corrupt hombres like McCain and—"

"Maybe. But it isn't all hogwash and hearsay, Loder. Listen. I brought you here to make a deal, not to argue the rights and wrongs. You can't deny that you've lived by the gun. I'm giving you a chance to use it now, but on the side of law and order."

"I'm listening, Governor. What's the deal?"

"Just this. I want *El Diablo* stopped. The rest are only small fry, and we'll get them eventually. But *El Diablo* is something else. I've tried all the conventional methods; lost some good men, too. Neither the Army nor the Rangers can spare men right now, with Santa Ana mustering troops again. I've got to clean my own house. All right, I aim to fight fire with fire. I'll use any means to hand to clean up Mesa County and put *El Diablo* where he belongs. Help me, Loder, and I'll see to it that you get a full pardon and a fresh start, with the slate wiped clean; even a section of land and enough cash to set you up in the cattle business, or anything else you've a mind to tackle. What do you say?"

"I'm still listening, Governor."

"That's it, Loder. What more can I say? Twin Rivers is the key to the whole business. I'm sure of it.

A hell-town, wide open, and run by people in cahoots with *El Diablo*. Big John Faulkner is still town marshal. He was a good man once, the best. And a friend of yours, I understand. But he's changed. Drinks too much, for one thing. I hear that's been partly your trouble, too, Loder. Faulkner's getting old and soft, the way I heard it. Perhaps you can shake him up and work something out between the two of you. I'm giving you this opportunity, Loder. The rest is up to you. You rode for the law once. I'm depending on you now. Don't let me down. I've been told I'm a fool to trust you with this assignment, that you've gone bad. The *Gazette* called you a cold-blooded killer without conscience or scruples. But I know how a man can get backed up against a wall with everything piling up. This is your chance to work things out, Loder."

"Sounds purty good," Loder had agreed. "I'm your huckleberry, Governor. I didn't murder Mannion, and I've been blamed for a lot of things I've never done. But likewise, there's plenty I ain't proud of, Kendrick, and I've often wished I could turn the clock back. I'll have a crack at smoking out this *El Diablo* sidewinder. But I'll want a free hand."

"There are no strings, Loder."

The governor had reached into a drawer and

removed a badge, which he had pinned on Loder's shirt.

"That makes it official," he had said. "It only remains for me to wish you good luck. Handle it any way you want, according to your conscience and common sense. I'm pleased you've decided to accept, if only for your father's sake."

An hour later, Loder had been ten miles from Austin, riding southwest. He recalled all this and, remembering the look on the bartender's flabby face, grinned wryly. He flipped ash from his quirly and fingered the badge again. It would come as a surprise to a lot of hombres, he thought, to see Reed Loder packing a U.S. marshal's star. He had made a hell of a start by killing Brice Ruskin. But the fool had left him no choice.

Loder got up from the bed and turned the key in the lock, then undressed and stretched out. Sleep was a long time coming, but when he did finally drift into oblivion he slept soundly.

## CHAPTER TWO

Loder awoke before sunup, washed and dressed and ate a substantial breakfast prepared by the bleary-eyed bartender, who was apparently responsible for almost every kind of chore around the place, in addition to serving behind the bar. The town was still quiet, the streets practically deserted, when Loder led his horse from the livery stable without disturbing the old man, presumably the hostler, lying asleep on a bunk in the lean-to shelter built onto the barn.

The storm had blown itself out during the night. The street was layered with drifted dust and grit. Doorways and alleys were choked with tumbleweeds. Loder mounted Satan and headed the animal toward the distant badlands, riding easily and allowing the big black to pick its own gait. The morning was fresh, the air filled with the fragrance of hill blossoms, of pine and juniper, and the tangy aroma of sagebrush. Rabbits and quail swarmed in the thickets.

Loder fashioned a quirly and let it droop from his lips. He struck a match, lit the weed and sucked smoke deep into his lungs. It was several years since he had seen Big John Faulkner, but he remembered the lawman well; at least the way Faulkner had been then. A top gunslinger in his day, Faulkner had enjoyed a reputation for toughness combined with fairness and integrity. Loder was no stranger to Twin Rivers. And he had heard trail talk about the town's decline, and Faulkner's, from various sources. Time was, Loder recalled, when Twin Rivers had been an orderly, peaceful place, tamed by Big John Faulkner. Now the town was, by all accounts, a haven for outlaws and renegade scum, run by a woman and a gambler named Burl Fadden. Between them they owned the saloon and most of Twin Rivers and, as Governor Kendrick had said, the place was used openly by *El Diablo*'s gang.

Loder had heard the talk about *El Diablo*, too. It was rumored that the raider was a Mexican, like most of his cut-throat crew. Other men claimed he was a white man, and it was alleged there was some connection between the outlaw and Kate Molloy, part-owner of the Border Queen Saloon. Loder knew Kate Molloy well. At one time they had been very close. Loder had even considered asking her to marry him. But that, too, had been a long time ago. They had drifted apart for various reasons, and Loder had not seen Kate for close to five years.

She had a brother, he remembered, the fastest man with a gun Loder had ever seen in action. In Laredo, he had seen Denton Molloy kill three men before two of the trio even cleared leather. That had happened soon after Loder joined the Rangers. A year later, an Indian scout reported finding a man who answered to Denton Molloy's description staked out over an ant-heap, spread-eagled, with his wrists and ankles bound with rawhide that had shrunk until the blackened strips were barely visible. The dead man's eyelids had been cut off, and he must have died hard. Kate had never gotten over it. Coyotes and buzzards and the ants had mutilated the corpse and eaten away most of the face, so that the body couldn't be positively identified. But the scout had found a letter written by Kate in the dead man's pocket, and that had seemed proof enough.

Thinking back, Loder sighed. He had often thought that he might have made a go of things with Kate Molloy if he hadn't met Molly Bergen. He remembered good times and recalled the kind of man Big John Faulkner had been. The marshal's downfall had been brought about by circumstances similar to Loder's personal ones, equally tragic. But whereas Molly Bergen had died from cholera, it was a stray bullet fired during a gun duel on Twin River's main street that killed Faulkner's wife, Judith, just a month after their daughter's fifteenth birthday. And Big John had fired that ricocheting bullet. Since then, like Reed Loder, the lawman had gone downhill, but more quickly and completely.

Now, if what Loder had heard was true, the former fire-eating marshal was a drunken bum, a mere pawn kept in office by Kate Molloy and her partner as long as it suited their nefarious ends. Kate, Loder knew, would do almost anything to make a fast dollar. He had always suspected that beneath that beautiful exterior was a mercenary little tramp. She had told him, when they last met, that she intended to get what she wanted from life, and the consequences be damned. And by all accounts she had come a long way since those days. But now, instead of sitting on the fence, she was on the wrong side of it.

Following her mother's tragic death, Ruth Faulkner had gone to live with her aunt in New Orleans. As far as Loder knew, she was still there. He remembered her as a gawky kid with pigtails and freckles. He drew at the quirly stub. The weed was cold, the end black. Loder swore and groped in his pocket for a match. Before Big John Faulkner had accepted the job of taming Twin Rivers, he had captained the same Ranger troop Reed Loder had ridden with. They had known good times together, rugged action and some tough situations. Loder didn't believe all he'd heard about the lawman, but he knew there was no smoke without fire, and since he had learned of Judith Faulkner's demise he had often started out to look up the marshal, but somehow had always been side-tracked.

Now Twin Rivers lay just a few miles to the south-west. And somewhere down there was the key to Kendrick's problem, and Loder's, the vital link that would reveal the identity of the murdering renegade who called himself *El Diablo*. Loder was tempted to remove the law badge and ride into town as plain Reed Loder, gunslammer. In the same breath he dismissed the notion. No, he decided, damned if he would skulk about like a sneaking coyote. He had undertaken to do a job, and he would do it. Besides, he had showed his hand back in San Rosa. Word would quickly get around that Reed Loder was gunning for *El Diablo* and wearing the badge of a U.S. marshal. All right. He would keep the star in plain view and, if necessary, back its authority with hot lead.

Gradually the terrain changed, became still bleaker, more barren. The brush thinned out. Soon Loder crossed the first of two dried-out creeks. Twenty years ago they had both held swift-flowing water, and it was from their junction that the town of Twin Rivers had derived its name.

It was past noon when Loder entered the sleepy town. There was very little activity. A lumbering wagon laden with ore and drawn by a team of dispirited mules rumbled down the main drag. Horses, tormented by swarming flies, were bunched along the street, mostly in front of the large saloon, The Border Queen. Most of the few men Loder passed seemed indifferent to his presence. A few regarded him with suspicion. But the sight of the badge aroused glowering hostility, and some degree of surprise that shortly yielded to sneering contempt. Lawmen were not welcome in Twin Rivers, but one man on his own was more of a joke than a threat.

Loder reined in near the saloon steps, dismounted and hitched Satan to the sagging rail. He slapped dust from his clothing with his hat, then eased his gun in leather—an instinctive, subconscious movement—and mounted the treads. A commotion sounded from inside, and he paused in the entrance, then pushed the batwings wide open when raucous laughter jarred harshly.

The spacious barroom was crowded. At the far end of the long bar, a shapely, dark-haired girl struggled in the powerful grip of a huge ox of a man. Close by, two other men, both roughly dressed and packing low-slung six-guns, stood grinning.

Abe Crudd, the big man, was chuckling as he pulled the girl against his gross body and tried to press his thick, fleshy lips to her dainty mouth. Crudd wore greasy range garb that reeked of animal dung and stale sweat. His girth was enormous, his build like that of a bear, squat and massive. His great limbs bulged with muscle. Long, shaggy, dirty-grey hair hung down over his reddened, close-set eyes. The girl's shirt-waist was torn, her flesh bruised where Crudd's fingers had gripped. She was pretty and young, not more than twenty. Reed Loder didn't recognize her right away. Neither did he know the tall, stooped figure occupying a chair a few feet away from Crudd.

Big John Faulkner had changed. When recognition finally came, Loder felt a distinct shock. The marshal was an old man, hunched, his face seamed and lined, eyes deeply sunken and ringed with dark shadow. His once-black hair was streaked with snowy white. He had a permanent twitch about the mouth, and his thin fingers shook uncontrollably as he brandished an almost empty whisky bottle and harangued Crudd and the two men with him in slurred, mumbling tones that brought more jeering laughter and put a scowl on Loder's grim face.

From Faulkner's drunken babbling Loder realized that the girl was the lawman's daughter, Ruth. Looking at her, he saw features that jogged his memory of her as a child. To everybody in the room the marshal was just a subject for cynical jest, a man old before his time, with all the fire and guts kicked out of him, or drowned in rotgut whisky. None of the score or more grinning onlookers made any attempt to help Ruth Faulkner. Near a curtained alcove, another woman, with a lovely face spoiled by a hard expression and a tight-lipped mouth, and with hair the color of ripe corn, stood leaning against the hand-rail at the foot of a broad staircase, smiling sardonically.

She turned her head slightly when Loder entered, and her eyes widened. Her lips parted, and she took an involuntary step forward, her mouth framing the gunfighter's name. At the top of the stairs, a tall, lean, darkly handsome hombre straightened from his leaning posture on the landing rail and quit grinning when he, too, saw Loder—and the law badge. Kate Molloy, the blonde woman, darted a swift glance toward the head of the staircase. Burl Fadden intercepted it and started down the stairs. Broad-shouldered, with a trim waist and flat hips, and wearing expensive broadcloth, Fadden was an imposing figure of a man. A pearl-handled Colt forty-four was holstered under his left arm, the butt just visible when his coat swung open. He was clean-shaven, his jet-black hair slicked back from a high forehead devoid of wrinkles.

The smile faded from Kate Molloy's face, too. Tall, and with a full but not overly-fat figure, she was decidedly attractive.

Nobody else noticed Loder for the time being. Crudd had the girl in a bear hug and was still attempting to trap her mouth with his. Every time Big John Faulkner tried to get up from his chair, one of Crudd's friends thrust him back again.

"Tame the li'l wildcat, Crudd," one of them encouraged. "She's been askin' for it."

"Don't think I won't," Crudd mouthed thickly, slobbering. He exerted greater pressure. "You'll be sorry you used that kind of talk to old Abe, gal. I sabe how to tame—"

"Let her go, you stinking hawg!"

The command snapped like a whiplash across the smoke-filled room. But it didn't register immediately on Crudd's slow mind. Loder repeated the order. This time Crudd heard him loud and clear. His lower jaw went slack. The smirk left his unshaven features. His huge body stiffened, tensed. Abruptly he released the girl, sent her stumbling toward her father, then turned slowly, scowling. Seeing Loder and the badge, he swore, then regained some of his composure and grinned derisively.

"Wal, now, look we've got here, boys," he jeered. "A two-bit lawman done come to town. Mebbe I didn't hear you right, drifter. You talkin' to me?"

"I was. And I still am. Are you hurt, Miss Ruth?"

The girl, with Big John Faulkner's arm round her waist, shook long hair back from her eyes. She stared at him. Ruth had inherited her mother's good looks and some of her father's former spirit.

"I'm all right," she answered sharply. "I'll fix you for that, Abe Crudd. You're too damned free with those dirty hands of yours. And you, stranger, how did you know my name? Who are you? You seem somehow——"

"Ask your dad. Touch that gun and I'll kill you, Crudd. I don't cotton to hulking skunks who manhandle women. The show's over, you men. Break it up."

Crudd hunched his shoulders aggressively. He spat into the strewn sawdust along the bar.

"You talk big, mister," he growled. "I don't need no gun to take care of you, whoever you are. You must be plumb loco, comin' in here and throwin' your weight about. We ain't got any use for lawmen in this here town, fella. And who the hell d'you think you're callin' a hawg, you long cow-son! I'll shove that tin star down your lousy throat."

"Don't try it, Crudd," the blonde woman warned. "That's Reed Loder—an old friend, and the fastest gun in the whole country. Hello, Reed. It's been a long time."

Loder nodded, but kept his calm gaze on Crudd.

"Hello, Kate," he answered. Big John Faulkner muttered. He peered at the gunslammer, put down the bottle.

"Reed Loder!" he mumbled. "Reed, boy, I sure—"

Abe Crudd wiped his coat sleeve across his face. Faulkner closed his mouth. Apparently the name Loder meant nothing to Crudd.

"I don't give a damn who he is," he growled. "I've seen two-bit gunslingers before—all wind and water. I'll bust his dad-blamed neck."

Abruptly he lowered his head and rushed at Loder with arms outstretched, ready to clutch and squeeze. Loder side-stepped adroitly, slammed a hard fist against the base of Crudd's thick neck, then grasped the man's arm and flung him against the wall with a force that brought dust showering down. Crudd, hurt and surprised, whirled, cursing, and rushed again. This time Loder stopped him with a punch that split Crudd's lips and brought a gush of spurting crimson. Blued steel rasped against oiled leather as one of the big man's friends drew a gun. Loder's hand dipped, so quickly it was less than a blur. Colt thunder crashed, reverberating through the room. Cursing men scrambled to get back out of the line of fire. Newt Bailey, the man who had pulled his weapon, spun round and fell against the bar, gripping a bullet-shattered right wrist. The other man, Shack Bonnatree, stared stupidly, fingers splayed above his holster, bewildered by the suddenness of it all.

A solid smacking sound echoed as Loder lashed out and rapped Crudd smartly over the head with the smoking gun barrel. The weapon was lined up on Bonnatree's belly before he recovered sufficiently from his surprise to complete his draw. Crudd, not completely stunned, dropped to one knee and slumped against the boards. He knelt there, holding his head and groaning.

"I warned you," Kate Molloy told him unsympathetically. "It was just high spirits, Reed. Crudd meant no harm."

"No? Depends how you look at it, Kate. He can think about it—in jail. You're still wearing a badge, Faulkner. I want Crudd and these other two jailed. Are you going to take them in, or must I do your job for you?"

Faulkner didn't answer. Kate frowned.

"Life's sure full of surprises," she remarked drily. "I never expected to see you back here, Reed, and wearing a badge. It doesn't add up. What are you doing in Twin Rivers, anyway?"

Loder gazed at her.

"I thought mebbe you'd have heard," he said. "I'm

back with the law, Kate. Just temporary, you might say. Fact is, I'm gunning for *El Diablo*. On your feet, Crudd."

Kate Molloy stared. She darted a keen glance at Fadden, who had halted midway down the stairs. She forced a laugh.

"You've been out in the sun too long, Reed," she said. "That kind of talk is calculated to get you killed. I won't deny I've heard of this *El Diablo*, and from what I hear he's bad medicine. If you think you can come here and flush him out by your lonesome, you're a bigger fool than I thought. And why come here, anyway? *El Diablo* operates in the badlands yonder. Nobody ever sees him. He doesn't bother us, and we don't bother him. Forget about him. It's good to see you. I mean that. I'm part owner of this place. See me later, and we'll talk. About old times, if you like, Reed."

"I might just do that, Kate. I've some questions I want to ask you."

Big John Faulkner quit the chair and lurched forward with hand outstretched.

"Reed, my boy," he said, his voice slurred, "couldn't hardly believe my eyes. Where'd you spring from? Ruth, honey, you remember Reed, surely?"

"I remember a gunfighter, Father, a cold-blooded killer who's made an evil reputation out of misery and death."

"Ruth! That ain't no way to talk about your dad's old friend. Shucks, gal, me and Reed was Rangers together. Times have sure changed, Reed."

Loder shook Faulkner's hand, though without enthusiasm.

"They sure have," he agreed coldly. "I heard you were having it kind of rough, John. But I didn't believe much of what I heard until now."

"Things ain't been easy, boy, since Judith died. But we can't talk here. Can't get over that badge, Reed. There's a powerful lot I want to say to you. Dad-burn it, you're a sight for sore eyes. Last person I expected to see in this stinkin' town. You'll come up to the house for supper, won't you? We can talk then, over a bottle. You'll have to forgive Ruth. I'm plumb obliged to you for hornin' in. Reckon I'm gettin' old and—"

"I'll be right pleased to come for supper, John. Right now I aim to see these hombres in jail. You're still town marshal. What are you waiting for?"

Faulkner straightened his stooped back. He stood swaying slightly. The gun at his hip and the tarnished star pinned to his vest seemed out of place, ludicrous. He ran unsteady fingers through his thinning hair.

"Damn right I'm the marshal," he growled. "I'm still the law in Twin Rivers, by thunder! Who do I have to jail, boy? And why?"

"Because I'm telling you, for one thing. And because it was your daughter Crudd was mauling. Stay on your feet. I remember when Big John Faulkner meant something around here. Get a hold on—"

"Why don't you leave him alone?" Ruth Faulkner demanded angrily. "What right have you to come here, ordering my father about? I don't know why you're wearing that badge. But on you it's a mockery. Oh, I'm thankful to you for peeling that swine off my back. But it isn't the first time I've put up with insults, and I don't suppose it'll be the last. Father is older and in poor health. You don't know what it's like living here, how it's been since my mother died. Leave him alone, please. Do you want to get him killed? He's old and tired and sick. If you scorn him into making a fool of himself, all you'll achieve will be to get him shot. You don't understand how it is here."

"I understand he's supposed to represent the law."

"The law. Who are you to talk about the law? An outlaw, with a price on your head. Anyhow, I'm not making any complaint against Crudd."

"You don't have to. I'm arresting him for assaulting a peace officer, and these other two men for assault with a deadly weapon. If your father hasn't got sand enough to make that star mean something any more, that's too bad, but I'm here to do a job, and there'll be some changes, believe me."

"Best listen to her, Reed," Kate Molloy advised. "It isn't like the old days. This is a tough town. My town, Reed, mine and Burl Fadden's. We like things the way they are, and we intend to keep them that way. If you're smart you'll climb on that horse of yours and make tracks out of here, back where you came from. You won't find who you're looking for here. But if you stay, he'll find you. Leave now, before it's too late."

She whirled on Crudd as he groped to his feet.

"I warned you, you big stupid ox!" she repeated. "Serve you right if he'd killed you."

Burl Fadden pushed past her. He confronted Loder. The tall gambler's bleak eyes regarded the gunfighter critically.

"I've been hearing a lot about you, Loder," he gritted.

"You're not wanted here. Kate's just given you some good advice, gunslammer. You might be hell on wheels, but I run this town. Start pushing, and you'll end up dead. You can't buck the odds, Loder. They're too long. And there's more than one way to skin a skunk. I'm telling you—"

Loder balled a hard fist and struck. The punch took Fadden flush in the mouth and hurled him back against the stairs. He sprawled on his back on the treads, knocked cold. Loder turned to face Faulkner.

"Well?" he asked. Some of the whisky fumes were clearing from the marshal's brain. He shook his head and squared his shoulders.

"No call to talk to me like that, Reed," he protested. "Mebbe I have sort of let things slide lately. But—"

He palmed his gun, threatening Bonnatree with the weapon.

"Get going, you hombres," he ordered. "I'll show you who's running this town, by grab!"

"Father!" Ruth objected. But Big John waved her aside.

"Reed's right, honey," he said. "It needed somebody like him to show me the way back. From now on things are going to be different around here."

Abe Crudd spat. He sneered defiantly.

"Why, you stove-up has-been," he jeered, "you just put your other foot plumb in the grave, Faulkner. How long d'you think you'll last now? You're living on borrowed time, along with this damn fool."

Loder pushed him toward the entrance. Crudd slouched forward. Faulkner, jabbing with his gun barrel, herded Bailey and Bonnatree across the floor. Bailey's face was chalk white. Blood dripped from between the fingers gripping his wrist.

"Get the sawbones," he gritted. "I'm bleedin' bad."

"You'll get attention," Loder told him. "Move."

Kate Molloy, standing over Burl Fadden's prone figure, stared after Reed Loger, anger mingling with admiration and respect in her expression.

"You fool," she muttered. "You blind, stubborn fool, Reed Loder."

# CHAPTER THREE

Burl Fadden sat erect and remained seated on the stairs, holding his bruised jaw and glowering. Kate Molloy bent and offered her hand to help him up, but he refused her help angrily, grasped the rail and hauled himself to his feet. The expression on his swarthy face was demoniacal.

"I'll kill that stinking gunslinger for this," he threatened. "Who the hell does he think he is? I'll fix his wagon, by Gawd, and quick."

"No!" Kate protested quickly. "I'll talk to him Burl, get him to leave town. We don't want any trouble with Reed Loder. And I don't want him harmed. I know your methods."

"Why? Are you still sweet on the long snake?"

"No, Burl. That was over a long time ago. But Reed Loder never did me a bad turn, far from it, and I don't want his murder on my conscience."

"Well, it won't burden my conscience any, by

thunder! The nerve of that damn saddle tramp, coming in here and bragging about what he's going to do, gunning for *El Diablo* and all. Who steered him to this neck of the woods, anyway? By Gawd, if it wasn't so durned insolent, it would be funny. But I ain't laughing, and neither will *El Diablo* be when he hears about it. We've got a good thing going here, and no two-bit drifter is going to horn in here, flashing a badge and acting tough. Hell, you've seen what he's capable of already—Abe whipped, and three of the boys behind bars. He's dangerous, and too damned handy with a gun. I'll take care of him, and I'll have Faulkner's hide, too, for his part in this. Until Loder showed up, that old fool's been a perfect front for us. And you say not to harm Loder?"

"And I'm still saying it. Don't underestimate him Burl. Reed Loder is more than dangerous, a fast gun. He's clever. But he's human, too. If you think anything about me at all, Burl, leave him alone. I'll talk to him, I promise. Maybe I can persuade him to line up with us. He'd be a good man to have, Burl, and he's been outlawed by the state these past months. That badge can't mean much."

"All right. Talk to the sidewinder. But you'd better make it stick. Loder's plumb poison, and right now I need a snooping lawman in here like I need a hole in the head. So get rid of him, and pronto, or else I will."

He sneered.

"I don't see anything clever in a man advertising his intentions that way," he added. "You'd think he'd have sense enough to curb his brag, if it is *El Diablo* he's after. And why the badge? How come a salty hellion like Loder is suddenly riding for the law and wearing the badge of a United States marshal? It doesn't stack up right to me, Kate. Ain't no hombre in his right mind would come here deliberately looking for the sort of trouble Loder can expect from *El Diablo*. That thieving lobo is as mean as they come, and you should know, by thunder, better than anybody. So what's Loder's game? Is he playing a lone hand? Or is there a Ranger troop holed up somewhere close? I don't like it one little bit. Even a man with Loder's reputation wouldn't be fool enough to think he could take over this town on his own. That badge is an open invitation to a bullet in the back."

"I don't know what he's up to, Burl. But I'll find out. Loder has always been a loner. Whatever he's here for, he must feel reasonably confident he can handle it alone. He always was that kind of man. It was inevitable that somebody would show up sooner or later, some outside law. It would have to be somebody like Reed Loder, if it is *El Diablo* he's after. Or maybe he's just talking big to make it look right to whoever pinned that star on his shirt. I'll sound him out, Burl.

Meanwhile, I want your promise that you'll stay out of his way and let me handle it."

Fadden shrugged. Kate turned and went up the stairs. Fadden watched her until she reached the landing, then moved toward the bar, reached for a bottle and a glass. He poured a generous drink, swallowed it and poured again, swore when one of the men crowding round joggled his elbow.

"Could be the law done got Loder out on a limb, Fadden," a thick-set, red-bearded man suggested. "He was worth five hundred bucks dead or alive last week. Now, suddenly, he shows up packin' a marshal's badge. That means they must have him under pressure, and he'll bust a gut tryin' to do whatever it is he came here to do. You'd best do somethin' about him real quick, Fadden. If you don't, and folks get the notion any stranger packin' a star can come in here raisin' hell, next thing you know we'll have trouble on our hands. Things have been buildin' up for quite a spell, Fadden, since we burned out them sodbusters."

"Gurney's right, Burl," another man agreed. "Loder's the thin edge of the wedge. You can't let him get away with anything."

"I don't aim to, Sawyer. Ben, tell Chase Croft I want to see him in my private office."

The bartender nodded. Fadden passed through a doorway beyond the bar and entered a large, com-

53

fortably furnished room. He took a cheroot from a silver-inlaid box on the heavy desk, bit the end off and was lighting the weed when there came a discreet knock on the door. It opened to admit a tall, thin man whose gaunt frame and deep-sunk eyes betrayed symptoms of advanced consumption. His narrow shoulders were hunched forward, his thinning hair streaked with grey. The bony fingers of his right hand hovered close to the black butt of the Colt forty-five holstered low against his sunken flank.

Chase Croft was a dying man. Everybody knew it except Croft himself. He refused to accept the fact, although the blood that often flecked his thin lips when he experienced one of his periodical coughing bouts should have convinced him. Croft was dying, but he himself dealt in death. A vicious, depraved hombre, fast with a gun and capable of any evil, he was useful to Fadden in many ways. Burl Fadden had his fingers in numerous pies that Kate Molloy knew nothing about, even though they were supposed to be partners. It wasn't only to protect his various interests and his property that Fadden employed a bunch of unscrupulous men, most of them petty thieves and gunslingers, any more than it was *El Diablo* who was responsible for all the hold-ups and rustling carried out in the area. Fadden wasn't content with a share of the gang's ill-gotten gains. There were some activities he felt best able to handle himself, with his own bunch. And it was Chase Croft, the cold-eyed, consumptive killer, who kept Fadden's men in line.

Despite the depravity and lawlessness in Twin Rivers, there were townspeople and tradesmen who stubbornly refused to move on, who persisted in their hope that some day things would change, that somebody like the man Big John Faulkner had once been would clean out Fadden and his hirelings and run them and Kate Molloy out of town. *El Diablo* had Twin Rivers in the cold grip of fear. His men used the town openly. No honest man and certainly no woman was safe on the streets after dark.

But by day life went on as usual. There was no school in Twin Rivers, no church. Few men with families to consider stayed in the town. But there were others, resentful and bitter men such as Carson Reeves, the storekeeper, and Josh Earl, the blacksmith, who had only themselves to think about, and who refused to abandon a lucrative business because of the evil they saw all around. Such men learned to close their eyes to much of what went on and to keep their mouths shut. The raiders from across the border were free spenders, and Twin Rivers lay directly in the path of the big trail herds drifting up from the Texas plains. Businessmen and shopkeepers did well and consequently developed hardened consciences. Yet most of them would have preferred to see the town the way it used to be, and the arrival of Reed Loder and his gunning of one of Burl Fadden's hirelings aroused considerable speculation and rumor.

The general consensus of opinion was that Loder was a brash fool who would be dead before the sun went down. Others respected his declared motives and spoke of a shrewd move by the Rangers to use Loder as a spy before sending men to tame the town. More level-headed men, such as Doc Haggerty, knew that the state had no peace officers to spare for civil duty, and that was the reason for giving the backing of a law badge to hombres like Reed Loder. Even so, the old adage about fighting fire with fire might work, and Doc and his friends debated the possibilities surrounding Loder's arrival with profound interest. Some of them were ready to back his play if necessary, once he had proved himself to be really on the side of law and order.

Big John Faulkner was a broken reed in whom the honest element had lost confidence. They pitied the marshal and his daughter. Meanwhile they watched and waited. But if Loder's arrival stirred up excitement, it also aroused cynicism, for what, the doubters asked, could one man do against not only Fadden and his crew but also against the sinister *El*

*Diablo* and his border wolves?

Chase Croft heeled the door of Fadden's office shut and leaned against it. A man of uncertain age, he had the look of a lean-gutted timber lobo. When he wiped bluish knuckles across his bloodless lips, protruding teeth scored faint white indentations along the back of his hand. His crumpled clothing was drab and stained. A flat-crowned black hat shadowed bleak, penetrating eyes.

"You sent for me, boss?" he asked. His voice was harsh, in keeping with his cadaverous figure and funereal garb. Fadden nodded and blew smoke toward the rafters.

"You know Reed Loder's in town," he said, "packin' a lawman's badge. I want him taken care of."

"But Kate said—"

"I don't give a damn what Kate said. I pay your wages, Croft. Loder's coming here constitutes a threat. I don't know how he's pinned *El Diablo* down to this territory, but he ain't just guessing. Mebbe he thinks he's holdin' aces. But I don't aim to let him or anybody else foul things up. So get rid of him."

"He's fast, Fadden; too fast for me, or anybody else in town. I dunno if—"

"There are ways, you fool. Right now he's over at the hotel getting slicked up before going to the

Faulkner place. We'll take care of Faulkner later. I'll l'arn him it don't pay to step out of line on the say-so of a two-bit gunslinger. But right now I'm more interested in stopping Loder before he stumbles onto something. Don't leave any sign that'll implicate me. Kate's got her uses. I'm not ready to toss her into the ashcan yet. Here; the usual bonus."

He took a wad of bills from a drawer, peeled off two fifties and tossed the money on the desk. Croft nodded and picked it up. He grinned, exposing foul teeth, thrust the money into the side pocket of his somber black coat, then opened the door and slouched from the room.

Along the street, in his room at the hotel, Reed Loder finished slicking back his long hair and put his hat on. He grinned at his reflection in the mirror. Clean-shaven and wearing a fresh shirt, he wasn't, he decided, a bad-looking hombre. The sight of Ruth Faulkner had given him a pleasant surprise. She had grown up, filled out, and was more woman than he had expected to see, woman enough to interest him in a way he found disturbing. There had been little room for women in his life, nothing of a permanent nature, ever. Thinking of Ruth, he stopped grinning. He had a chore to do, and until it was accomplished he had no time for anything else. His whole future depended on the success of his mission. He dared not fail; neither could he afford to clutter his mind with vague longings and sentimental thoughts. All the same, having supper with Ruth would be a pleasant change from bacon and beans warmed over a campfire.

He picked up his gunbelt and was slapping it round his lean waist when the sound of footsteps furtively approaching the door of his room brought a scowl to his face. He hadn't expected Fadden to make a hostile move so soon. The shuffling tread stopped. A board creaked. Loder heard a muffled oath and grinned mirthlessly. Steel whispered against leather as he palmed his gun. The door handle turned. Somebody thrust his weight against the wood. The door opened a crack. Loder stepped quickly and quietly to one side and stood with the six-gun held poised.

Abruptly, a booted foot smashed the door wide open with a force that caused it to crash against the wall. A tall, gaunt figure loomed, crouching, gun extended, chopping down in the instant that Chase Croft glimpsed Loder's shadowy form. Loder's calloused thumb lifted from the hammer spur. Flame stabbed the semi-gloom. Lead smacked into Croft's lunging body, tore through flesh and sinew into his heart and hurled his bony frame back through the doorway. Dead on his feet, he slammed against the wall. The gun fell from his relaxing grasp and skated across the boards. He sagged, open-mouthed, eyes

59

bulging horribly. Blood, welling from the hole in the front of his grey shirt, soaked the drab material and spread quickly.

Loder punched the spent shell from his weapon, replaced it with a fresh load, leathered the gun and stood looking down at the huddled figure. A few heads thrust from doorways along the corridor. A fat man emerged from the room adjoining Loder's, took one startled look, then withdrew hastily. Doors slammed. White faces were withdrawn. But Loder felt the impact of staring eyes watching his every move. Feet clumped on the stairs. The elderly man who managed the hotel for Burl Fadden lumbered onto the landing and along the hallway, puffing and complaining.

"What's goin' on here?" he demanded. "More of your damn snake work, Loder? You ain't—"

Loder wound strong fingers into the front of the man's thick flannel shirt and shoved him up against the boards.

"Not so free with your flabby mouth, friend," he warned. "That skinny varmint tried to cut a rusty. Who is he?"

The man's eyes widened with fear. He gulped and licked his lips. Two other men who had followed him up the stairs checked their advance and stood silently by, staring.

"I asked you a question," Loder said, shaking the

fat man.

"Croft, mister. Chase Croft. What d'you expect, flashin' that badge? There's men in this town who don't cotton to lawmen, Loder, especially—"

Loder banged him against the wall.

"Just remember I am wearing this badge," he snapped. "And there's plenty of room in the jail yonder. Who's Croft? One of Fadden's pet rattlers?"

"Sure, Chase worked for Burl Fadden. 'Most everybody in town works for Fadden, one way or another, either for him or for Kate Molloy. There'll be more'n Chase Croft after your hide, Loder, if you stay around here."

Loder released the man and pushed past the others.

"What'll I do with him?" the fat man demanded angrily, indicating the corpse.

"Get the medico over here. He'll take it off your hands. Or tote it over to Fadden's place yourself."

Loder descended the stairs and shoved the street door open. He went out into the failing sunlight and turned south along the dusty street, making for The Border Queen. Men stared as he entered the saloon. Some of them hurriedly finished their drinks and departed. Others huddled together, conversing in low tones. Many a hand dropped toward a gun butt as Loder strode toward the bar.

"Where's Fadden?" he demanded. Ben Stole, the

barkeep, shrugged.

"I ain't Burl Fadden's keeper," he answered sullenly. Loder reached over the counter, grabbed Stole's shirt front and jerked him forward.

"I asked you a question, fella," the rangy gunfighter snapped. "Mebbe you'd like them snaggle teeth shoved down your throat? Where's Fadden?"

"I don't know, damn you! I ain't seen him since he went upstairs with Kate Molloy."

Loder released him, and Stole straightened his crumpled clothing angrily. Loder started up the stairs. A man standing in a corner drew his gun, but the man beside him gripped his wrist and rammed his friend's weapon back into the holster.

"Don't be a fool, Sam," he warned. "That sidewinder's got eyes in the back of his head. Fadden'll take care of him, or *El Diablo* will. No call to risk our hides."

At the top of the stairs, Loder hesitated. A dozen doors opened off the wide landing. One of them swung wide as he stood there, and his gun came into his hand with bewildering speed.

"You planning to shoot me, Reed?" Kate Molloy asked. She was smiling, standing hip-shot in the doorway with one slim hand resting on the upright, the other holding a half-filled glass. She wore a flimsy robe over lacy undergarments.

"Where's Fadden?" Loder demanded.

"How should I know?"

"He ain't here with you?"

"At this time of day? Come in and see for yourself. I want to talk to you, anyway. I haven't seen Burl for half an hour or more. I don't know where he is. What do you want with him?"

"He sent one of his hired guns to the hotel to toss lead in my craw, a jasper named Chase Croft. He won't be coming back."

"Croft? You killed him?"

"It was him or me. And I've a few questions to ask Fadden."

Kate frowned.

"So have I," she said pointedly. "He promised me—well, never mind. Croft probably acted on his own initiative. Lawmen aren't popular in Twin Rivers, Reed. Come in."

She held the door open invitingly. Loder hesitated. Kate grasped his arm and drew him inside. She closed the door, seated herself on the edge of a large bed and sat dangling her legs. She patted the covers.

"Come and sit down," she insisted. "You make me nervous, standing there."

Loder hooked a chair close with his boot toe and sat on it with his arms folded on the high back.

"You said you wanted to talk," he said. "So talk.

Not that we've anything to talk about, Kate."

Kate stood up, moved toward him, leaned over and kissed him on the mouth.

"I'm sure we can think of something," she answered, smiling. "Like, for instance—how would you like to ride out of here with five thousand dollars in gold in your saddle-bags?"

Loder pulled a green bandana from his coat pocket and deliberately wiped his lips where Kate's had left crimson smears.

"Don't try to sidetrack me, Kate," he told her. "It won't work. I came here to do a job. I gave my word. And I intend to keep it."

"It's that important?"

"Yes. It can mean a fresh start, a whole new life. I can't afford to pass it up. You can't buy me off, Kate, and Fadden can't scare me off. I aim to nail *El Diablo* any way I can."

"Alone? You're crazy! Listen to me, Reed. Whatever they promised you, it's no use to a dead man. You know you can't win."

"I can try. You're no fool, Kate. You must see where all this is bound to end. Why not quit while you're ahead? Help me, and you help yourself. It's not too late. I found that out. It's never too late."

Kate laughed. But there was bitterness underlying the mocking sound.

"Would it do any good?" she asked. "Suppose I did break with Burl Fadden? What if I did help you? Would it make any difference, between you and me, I mean? Would it?"

"No, it wouldn't. I'm sorry, but that part of my life is a closed book. You made your bed a long time ago, Kate. Now you'll have to—"

"But, Reed, Burl Fadden means nothing to me. You've got to believe that. Oh, I was attracted to him once, and we get along well enough most of the time. But I've never loved any man but you. I loved you then, and I still do. I haven't changed."

"I have. So have a lot of things. I'm through hiding, Kate. I'm sick of watching my back-trail, never knowing when I'll get a bullet in the back. I accepted this badge because it was the only way to wipe the slate clean. I'm giving you a chance to do the same. Cut loose from Fadden and help me nail *El Diablo*, and—"

"I can't. You don't understand. It isn't that simple. Why must you be so stubborn? And who are you to preach? You fool! Are you so blind that you can't see I'm trying to save you from your own folly? It isn't me who's in danger, Reed. It's you! If Fadden doesn't kill you, *El Diablo* or his men will. You can't—"

"So you do know *El Diablo*. How well do you know him, Kate?,' The question came like a pistol shot, probing relentlessly. But Kate refused to be trapped.

"I didn't say I knew him," she countered. "I know of him. He could walk the streets of Twin Rivers every day without anybody knowing who he was. But everybody hereabouts knows his reputation. Don't try to implicate me, Reed Loder. I know no more about *El Diablo* than is common knowledge, and that isn't much, only hearsay, mostly. Sure, his men come and go as they please in this town. But they don't steal from us, and we don't bother them. I run a saloon, Reed. I don't care who drinks my liquor so long as they pay for it."

"And it doesn't matter if they pay with stolen money, or gold with blood on it?"

Kate shrugged.

"I lost any scruples I had years ago," she answered. "I like the kind of life I lead, and only one thing would persuade me to swap it for something else. You know what that is. If I can't have it, then you're just wasting your time, Reed."

"So are you, Kate. I'll do what I came for in spite of you and Fadden. Don't get in my way."

"And if I do?"

Loder didn't answer. He merely shrugged, then stood up.

"Go on then," Kate said angrily. "Get yourself killed. I've said my piece. If you won't listen to reason, you'll have to take the consequences. I can't protect you from yourself. Now you'd better leave."

Loder nodded. He moved to the door and opened it. As he stepped over the threshold into the corridor, he saw the shadow of an uplifted arm and a hand holding a gun on the wall. He leaped back instinctively, reaching for his own weapon, but was too late to avoid the downward swing of a slashing gun barrel. The blow dazed him, numbed his limbs, and he fell with lights flashing before his eyes, a black fog threatening to engulf his seething brain. The gun he had drawn was kicked from his grasp. A tall figure loomed. The sound of a cocking gun hammer penetrated Loder's clouded consciousness.

Impulsively, Kate Molloy lunged at the intruder, clutching at his arm. She dragged him away from Loder's sprawled figure.

"No, Saul!" she commanded. "Put that gun away. Please! I can't let you kill him in cold blood."

Saul Morrow, another of Fadden's hirelings, stood hesitantly with the six-gun pointing at Loder's head.

"Fadden said to finish him," he argued. "He gunned Chase Croft and—"

"Don't argue with me. I'll have no shooting in my place. He's Burl's problem. Settle it outside, not in here. Get out!"

Morrow, stoop-shouldered, unshaven and shifty-eyed, scowled. His thumb rocked the gun hammer.

"I dunno," he answered. "Fadden ain't goin' to like it if I don't do like he says."

"I'll handle Burl. I asked him to leave Loder to me, and he agreed. So get out. Now!"

Reluctantly, Morrow obeyed, but paused to pick up Loder's forty-four from the floor. Morrow was cut from the same slab as Chase Croft, a ruthless human lobo without pity or scruples, quick to seize an unfair advantage, a man with a low mentality, unable to think for himself. But he could handle a gun, and Fadden had use for such men. In the doorway, Morrow turned, still undecided, and stared at Kate. She returned his sullen gaze.

"All right," he snarled. "Have it your way. It don't make a heap of difference to Fadden, I reckon, whether I kill that badge-totin' skunk in here or outside. Seems Fadden was right about you still carryin' a torch for that gunslammin' hellion. But I aim to quench it plumb permanent. You tell Loder I'll be waitin' on the street for him. He'll have to come out sometime, and when he does I aim to blow his fool head off. And remember, Kate—if he just happens to have a gun when he shows his face, we'll sabe quick enough where he got it."

Viciously, he drove his boot against Loder's ribs, then thrust the confiscated six-gun inside his belt and slouched from the room.

# CHAPTER FOUR

When the mental fog finally cleared from Reed Loder's head and he realized who the woman bending over him was, he swore. He sat up, sagged against the door frame and clutched at it, gasping. He focused bleary eyes on Kate Molloy.

"Well?" she asked. "Are you convinced now? You came closer to Boothill than any man has any right to get and still be alive. You've got me to thank that you aren't lying there with a hole through your skull."

She helped him to his feet. Still rubbery-legged, Loder stood unsteadily, blinking, wincing when pain lanced his sore, swollen scalp.

"What happened?" he demanded thickly, fingering the large lump on the side of his head.

"You mean you don't remember? Somebody tried to kill you, that's all. And he would have, too, if I hadn't talked him out of it."

"Another of Fadden's sidewinders?" Loder asked.

"That partner of yours doesn't miss a trick, does he? And you're up to your purty neck in the same dirty business."

He bent, picked up his hat and put it on, swearing again when the band pressed against the swelling. The thick felt had absorbed some of the blow, which otherwise would have split his skull wide open. His hand strayed to his empty holster.

"I suppose I should thank you for saving my life," he said. "All right, I am thanking you. Mebbe there's hope for you yet."

He started along the corridor.

"Wait!" Kate called sharply. "He's out there on the street, waiting for you. The moment you go out you're dead, Reed. You'd best go out the back way."

"Who was it? Fadden?"

"Saul Morrow. One of Burl's—er, wagoners. Oh, Reed! Why won't you listen to me? There's too much at stake here. Fadden can't afford to let you live unless you throw in with us. How long can you hope to keep on? I just saved your life. Why must you throw it away?"

"I can't answer that, Kate. Dying doesn't come easy to any man. But if that's in the cards, then that's how it'll have to be. Life doesn't mean all that much to me, anyhow. But I'll sure as hell go down fighting."

"Like just now, with some man standing over you

with a gun aimed at your head, and you lying there unconscious? Why fool yourself, Reed? You can't fight Burl Fadden alone, and you don't have a ghost of a chance against *El Diablo*. I won't fight you, Reed, you know that. But—"

"All right, then help me. You can help me to cheat Boothill a while longer by giving me a gun."

"A gun? I don't have one, leastways not here, in my room. In Burl's office, maybe. But if—"

"Forget it. Tell Fadden I'll be back."

Steadier on his feet now, he moved quickly along the corridor and reached the back stairs, descended them and gained the street door without being seen. Once in the alley, he had the choice of going to left or right, but either way would bring him out onto the main drag, and the wooden fence backing the narrow street was all of fifteen feet high. Frowning, Loder kept walking, taking the left turn. He had a spare six-gun in the saddle-bag in his hotel room. His head ached abominably. But his brain was clear again, and alert.

Another fifty yards and he would be mounting the hotel steps. He had taken thirty paces and had less than twenty-five to go when a man he knew instinctively was Saul Morrow slouched from a gloomy opening and stood straddle-legged with drawn gun dangling loosely in his grasp, grinning wolfishly as he

71

awaited Loder's approach. The gun barrel came up, stopping on a level with Loder's belly. Morrow eared back the hammer.

"That'll be far enough, lawman," he mouthed. "Always hankered after killin' me a U.S. marshal, Loder. Reckon this is as far as you go, hard hombre."

Loder stopped. He held his coat open.

"I ain't packing a gun," he said. Morrow's grin broadened.

"I know," Morrow answered. "I've got it, Loder, right here. It was me put that crease in your skull just now. Aimed to finish you then, gunslammer, but Kate objected to blood on the carpet. Haw! I reckon there's dust a-plenty out here to soak up every last drop."

It was Loder's own gun that Morrow held. His grin faded.

"How d'you want it, Loder?" he asked harshly. "In the belly—or between the eyes?"

Loder stared around. He was trapped, and there seemed no way out. Men were bunched along the street. Outside the general store, just a few yards from where Loder stood, Ruth Faulkner sat beside her father on the high seat of a buckboard laden with supplies. Her face was pale. Big John Faulkner held the reins, so tightly that his knuckles gleamed white. He seemed like a man in a trance, his mouth gaping loosely, his eyes staring fixedly. Fading sunlight gleamed dully on the tarnished symbol of his supposed authority. Nobody made a move to stop Morrow from committing murder. His thumb was lifting off the hammer spur when Ruth Faulkner suddenly lashed out with the whip she held and flicked the lash across the rump of the nearest of the buckboard team, causing the animal to rear and plunge.

For an instant, Morrow's attention, like that of everybody else, was distracted. And in that moment the girl threw down the whip, snatched the six-gun from her father's holster and tossed it to Loder with desperate strength. Loder, already slewing sideways, caught the weapon deftly and whirled, the hard edge of his left-hand palm chopping against the hammer spur. Gun thunder reverberated along the quiet street—three shots, fired so close together they sounded like one continuous report.

Saul Morrow was spun round, flung backwards like a jerking puppet and smashed against the wheel of a stationary wagon. His gun blasted harmlessly into the dirt. Then he was sagging down, with a dribble of blood oozing from his nostrils and a dark stain spreading across the front of his calfskin vest. His sightless eyes were open, staring glassily, but he was dead even before the third shot ripped away the back of his head.

Loder approached the dead man, flopped the body

over with the toe of one boot, bent and retrieved his gun from where Morrow had dropped it. He checked it over briefly, holstered it, then pushed through the gaping crowd toward the Faulkners' buckboard. He held out the marshal's six-gun. Faulkner took it automatically.

"I'm mightly obligated to you, Miss Ruth," Loder said. The girl looked at him. She didn't smile.

"You did me a favor," she answered curtly. "Now we're even. If you're coming to supper, you'd best get your horse and ride out with us. We live a good way out of town—or maybe you don't remember?"

"I remember all right. And thanks again."

"No thanks necessary. I couldn't just sit there and let that man murder you. You were foolish to come back here, Reed Loder. You'll be an even bigger fool if you stay. Burl Fadden and that Molloy woman run this town. It's nothing but a haven for thieves and murderers since Father's illness. You always were a stubborn man, Reed Loder. Think over what I've said. We'll be moving along. You can catch up with us. But remember you're my father's guest, not mine. I'd sooner you stayed away from us. All you'll bring us is trouble."

"I reckon it's a mite late to think about that," Loder said. "You siding me against Fadden's gunslinger that way—he won't forget that."

"Pay no heed to her, Reed," Big John intervened. "Don't add to my shame, gal. She means no harm, Reed. She doesn't understand. Gawd help me, I'm to blame. I just sat there, unable to do a damn thing, watchin' Morrow shapin' to kill you. I reckon the whisky must have addled my brains, boy. Reed's my friend, Ruth. You treat him as such. And you fork that bronc of yours and hustle out to the homestead, Reed."

"I'll be along, soon as I've had a word with the sawbones."

Faulkner nodded. He picked up the whip his daughter had dropped and started the team moving. Loder watched the buckboard jolting on its way, turn the bend at the end of the street and head toward the hills. The Faulkner home, he remembered, lay in a timbered valley about six miles northwest of town. Big John had often said that some day he would turn in his star and take up farming. The homestead was in an ideal situation. Loder sighed. His own roots were in the land.

A big, florid-faced man wearing a somber black frock coat and a high, hard hat was limping across the street, black bag in hand. Dr. Eli Haggerty wasn't a man to waste words. His brusque manner was misleading, for he was actually a sincere, warm-hearted man, but living in Twin Rivers had taught him caution and soured his nature. He nodded a curt greeting.

"That badge," he said. "What's it stand for, Loder?"

"You see it," Loder replied.

"I see a gunslammin' hellbender wearin' the badge of a U.S. marshal, that's what I see. I've heard of you, Loder. Knowed your dad, way back. The way I heard it, you ain't a hombre who scares easy. That's good, because this town needs a good lawman, if you're on the square, and there's still some folks who ain't afraid to put Fadden and his buzzards in their place, given the right kind of leadership. I'm Doc Haggerty, sawbones, coroner, and undertaker, too. Never hard up for business in this town, by thunder! Don't let Fadden spook you out of Twin River, Loder. Mebbe we can get together later on for a talk. You ridin' out to the Faulkner place?"

"I reckon, although I'll allow that gal of his made it purty plain I'm plumb poison."

"Ruth don't mean it. She's had it purty rough lately. Watch out for more snake work, Loder. Fadden's more treacherous than a sidewinder."

"I'll do that," Loder told him. He left the medico and approached the livery stable. Satan, enjoying a feed of oats, resented being disturbed and tried to take a piece out of Loder's shoulder, but the Texan, used to such exhibitions of temper, avoided the yellow teeth and curbed the animal with his customary tact. He saddled up, mounted and quit the alley at a fast run. The buckboard had a fair start, but was moving slowly, and he overtook it rapidly. Big John, sobered by the clean, fresh air, was talkative, continually harping back to the old days. The girl maintained a tight-lipped silence, only answering, curtly, when she was spoken to directly. She obviously disapproved strongly of Loder, or at least of his influence on her father.

Several times Loder, twisting in the saddle, caught her staring at him with mingled resentment and confusion in her gaze. But they both respected the aging marshal's eagerness and childlike pleasure at seeing Loder again. Ruth, while unable to understand her father's depth of feeling for a gunfighter with Loder's reputation, nevertheless appreciated that Loder must have some good qualities, or at least he must have had at one time, for her father had always chosen his friends carefully in the past, and he would hear no criticism of the former Texas Ranger. Obviously, Ruth realized, Loder must possess qualities of which she was in ignorance. Her memory of him was hazy, of a reckless, clean-limbed kid with a quick smile. The cold-eyed man riding ahead of the buckboard was a stranger, a gunfighter and a killer, even though he now wore the badge of a lawman.

Ruth frowned, displeased by her undeniable interest in Loder. Whatever he was, he had saved her from a mauling at Abe Crudd's hands. The least she could do in return was to be civil. She sighed. Loder seemed bent on causing trouble, and she was afraid of how the repercussions would affect her father, and what the outcome of her own impulsive act would be. For months she had tried to persuade her father to leave Twin Rivers. But until Reed Loder showed up, Burl Fadden had maintained too strong a hold over Big John Faulkner. Perhaps, Ruth thought, she should be grateful for Loder's intervention, for his creating a showdown situation. Maybe he could persuade her father to quit, and spare him further mockery and shame.

She was still engrossed in her brooding thoughts when the buckboard turned off the trail onto Faulkner land. The long, squat house was strongly built of logs chinked with adobe, and roofed with large shingles. Towering cottonwood trees overshadowed the place. A pleasant setting. To the west a shallow creek flowed, and brush grew green and dense against a background of sweeping hills. It was ideal farming country. Yet there would never be any farm, Ruth knew, and no settlement or peace of mind so long as Fadden and his equally ruthless mistress ran Twin Rivers, and *El*

*Diablo* and his owlhoot bunch dominated the border town.

Perhaps somebody like Reed Loder was necessary to bring about a change, somebody who was capable of fighting evil with evil. Not that Loder looked evil. He was, Ruth had to admit, a strikingly handsome man, little altered in appearance since she had last seen him, so long ago.

The buckboard creaked to a halt in front of the verandah steps. A gangling hired man named Garrond led the team away. Inside, the simple but comfortably furnished house seemed more roomy and spacious than it appeared from the trail. The bareness of the walls was offset by bear, deer, and cougar pelts and by an assortment of weapons. Buffalo hides covered the floor. A Springfield rifle with silver inlaid stock and beautifully chased barrel and breech occupied a place of honor over the stone fireplace. Twenty years ago, Big John Faulkner had won that rifle against all comers in a state-wide shooting contest.

Once inside, the marshal promptly produced a bottle of whisky and two glasses, then seated himself at the solid table. Loder removed his hat and gunbelt and sat opposite him. Faulkner poured, filling both glasses to the brim. He fired questions at Loder. Ruth busied herself in the adjoining kitchen. Presently the savory smell of frying steak permeated the house, mingling with the aroma of freshly ground coffee. Shadows were lengthening. Eventually Ruth lit a large brass kerosene lamp suspended by chains above the table. Loder, relaxed by the whisky, enjoyed a prime cheroot and conversed with Faulkner, whenever he could get in a word.

Ruth laid the table and presently brought the food, steaming hot, on large earthenware dishes. Despite a feeling of awkwardness prompted by the girl's coldness and aloof manner, Loder ate heartily. Ruth was a good cook. Her father merely toyed with his food, but drank whisky with a regularity that brought a frown to his daughter's face. Conversation flagged during the meal. Afterwards, Faulkner announced his intention of smoking a pipe of tobacco on the porch. Loder, wanting a chance to speak with Ruth alone, said he would join the marshal presently. Faulkner went outside, leaving the door ajar.

Loder helped Ruth clear away the greasy dishes. She preceded him into the kitchen, put down her load and was about to return for more when Loder grasped her arm.

"Look," he said, "can't we be friends? All right, so you don't like what I am, leastways what I've been. I'm none too proud of it myself; that's one reason why I'm wearing this badge. For whatever it's worth, I'm

through with gunslinging, finished with the old life.
When I rode with your dad, things were different. I
never rightly figured out how I got side-tracked after I
quit the Rangers, or why I quit. I've regretted it.
There's a lot I'm sorry for. But all that's in the past."

Ruth removed his fingers from her arm.

"I'd like to believe that," she told him. "But how
can I, with two dead men back at Doc Haggerty's
place? Who is it behind that badge—a lawman or a
gunfighter? There was a time when I liked you, Reed,
as a person. I was very young then, but there are
things I remember. I've often thought about you. I
used to think about you quite often, wondering what
had become of you, hoping you'd come back some
day. Then I began to hear rumors. But I didn't believe
them, not at first. Even when I could no longer close
my eyes to the truth, I tried to make excuses for you,
until I finally ran out of excuses and realized you had
become what people said—a hired gunman. And now
you have come back, with a gun and a badge. But
you're not welcome, Reed Loder. You're trouble, any
way you look at it."

"Not for you, Ruth, or your father. I'm sorry you
feel that way. It ain't never too late to start afresh, and
now I've been given the chance. There's a pardon goes
with this star, and that ain't all. I know I'm only
wearing this badge because they reckon I'm ex-

pendable. Dawg eat dawg, and if Reed Loder gets his ticket to Boothill in the process, wal, who cares? Kind of ironic, ain't it? A week ago I was wanted for murder. It wasn't murder, but that was what they called it. Now, because they need a fast gun and can't spare regular lawmen, suddenly they're willing to make a deal, and your 'murderer' winds up a U.S. marshal. Wal, I aim to fool them. I intend to do the job they sent me here to do, and earn that pardon.''

"Fine sentiments, Reed. But what can you hope to do against Fadden's crowd and that Molloy woman? Everybody knows they're in cahoots with the murdering renegade who calls himself *El Diablo*. I admire courage. But what you're attempting to do is madness. Until you came back we were at least able to live here, Father and I, without too much pressure and friction. But now—well, after today only God knows what will happen, or what Fadden's men will do to Father. I'm not concerned about myself. But he's getting old, and he's been through so much. If they harm him, perhaps even kill him, it'll be your fault. How can you ask me to be your friend?''

"Mebbe I don't have the right. But I am asking all the same. You're looking at this all wrong. Grief and hard liquor have cost your dad his place in this community. He was my friend, and he still is. But there ain't no use trying to whitewash the facts.

Fadden's gotten him over a barrel, and the longer Big
John continues to knuckle under, the harder it'll be
for him to regain his self-respect. I aim to bust this *El
Diablo* sidewinder's bunch, and I'll break Fadden,
and Kate Molloy, too, if they get in my way. If I can
get a few of the decent element behind me, I will nail
that damned renegade, and no two ways about it. I
want to help your dad get back on his feet before it's
too late. If you care for him, instead of trying to shelter
him, you'll want him to be the kind of peace officer he
used to be."

"I'd rather just keep him alive."

"Sure you would. But that's a purely selfish
viewpoint. What about him? What d'you think all this
is doing to him? Don't tell me he's changed that
much, that he likes licking Fadden's boots. Hell! I've
seen him de-horn three killers without firing a shot
and put faster men than I'll ever be in a Boothill
grave. I've seen him whip hombres twice his size. That
was Big John Faulkner. Did you ever stop to think why
he allowed Fadden to back him into this situation? It's
you he's thinking of. He's afraid of what will happen
to you. That's why he's willing to take all the insults
and humiliation. Yet there's still a vestige of pride that
won't let him quit and run. It's always easier to bend
with the wind than to resist it. He started out making
excuses, too. Now he's got to a state where he can t

resist without help. Whisky is a powerful enemy,
Ruth. But you're content to see him grovel, to see
Fadden and scum like Crudd make a mockery of
everything your father once stood for. I'm telling you,
a man like Big John would rather be dead, though
he'll never admit it to you. It's killing him as surely as
the whisky or anything Fadden can do to him."

Ruth stared, shocked by the bluntness of his speech.

"So you're suggesting I stand by and let him go to
his death in a blaze of stupid glory?" she retaliated.
"You're saying that's what he'd rather do? Even
though he wouldn't stand a chance, you think he
would fight Burl Fadden and the rest if it wasn't for
me?"

"That's part of it. Whisky helps him to salve his
conscience. Today he regained a fraction of his self-
respect. You've seen how he's been since then, pleased
with himself, with you, feeling that perhaps he's still
more than just a bad joke. He's still got it in him,
Ruth. Don't stifle it. Trust me. Let me help him to
fight back. Because with or without his backing, I aim
to get to *El Diablo* through Fadden. And after what's
happened, it's too late for your father to back down
now."

"Yes," she agreed. "It is, thanks to you and to my
own folly, if indeed saving the life of any man can be
considered folly. I think perhaps I've misjudged you.

But despite all you've said, I'm going to try to persuade Father to leave here, right away, in the morning. What you do is your affair. I'm only concerned with what's best for—"

"I heard that, Ruth," her father broke in, appearing suddenly in the doorway. "Thought you said you'd be right out, Reed. I've been sittin' there, listenin' to the pair of you, and I don't mind tellin' you, Ruth, a lot of what Reed says makes good sense. He's right, by thunder! I am sick of eatin' Fadden's dirt. I dunno what's gotten into me lately. But I do know it's goin' to be different from now on. I was about ready to kick over the traces before Reed showed up, honey, so don't go blamin' him for everythin'. I've been a damn fool, Ruth. It needed somebody like Reed Loder to jolt some sense back into me. And it ain't no use you lookin' at me that way. My mind's made up. I'm through with eatin' crow."

He looked at the half empty bottle gripped in his gnarled right hand, then suddenly hurled it savagely against the wall.

"To hell with the whisky, too," he growled. "I'm plumb sick of sittin' around feelin' sorry for myself. Time was when I felt too proud to wear this star. Wal, like Reed says, it's never too late to start afresh. I'll back your play, boy. You name it, and by cracky, Big John Faulkner'll do it. Pour me another cup of that coffee, daughter."

Ruth looked at him, then at Loder. Her shoulders sagged. She sighed audibly.

"Perhaps I have been selfish and thoughtless," she admitted, "like an ostrich hiding its head in the sand. I suppose it is time somebody stood up to Fadden, and that butchering fiend, *El Diablo*. But I'm so afraid for you, Father. You're not a young man any more, and—"

"Shucks, ain't nothin' goin' to happen to me, honey. It's the whisky. It does things to a man, sort of slows down his thinkin'. But I can still unlimber a shootin' iron along with the best of 'em, I reckon. Only need a little practice and I'll—"

"That's loco talk, and you know it," Loder interrupted. "A shotgun's a heap more persuasive. I need somebody to watch my back, John, that's all. Fadden won't expect a lot of resistance from you. Mebbe I can use him to get at *El Diablo*. All I want you to do is stay close to the jailhouse and discourage any attempt to bust Fadden's men loose. There'll likely be others joining Crudd and the rest. If you make a stand against Fadden now, a few more will probably follow your lead. Doc Haggerty's strong for law and order. He favors a vigilante movement. There must be others who feel the same way who'll show their hand once Fadden's back is to the wall."

"You make it all sound very convincing," Ruth

said. "I'm beginning to revise my opinion of you. You're a strange man, Reed Loder, with a glib tongue. You should have been a politician. Doc Haggerty's an old fire-eater. But even a dozen like him wouldn't be a match for Fadden's gunslingers."

"Let it ride," her father said. "We'll think of somethin'. Right, Reed? You used to play a fair hand of poker, boy. We've time for a few hands before bed, I reckon."

# CHAPTER FIVE

Reed Loder stayed the night at the Faulkner place. He ate an early breakfast, and an hour after sunrise was riding back to town with Big John Faulkner, fully expecting Fadden's men to have released their sidekicks from jail. They found the jailhouse as the marshal had left it, the prisoners sullen and complaining. Evidently Fadden had decided to let them sweat it out for a while.

"Fadden will have your scalp for this, Faulkner," Crudd greeted Big John. "You must have gone plumb loco. If you're smart, old man, you'll let us outta here right now, before the rest of the boys tear this two-bit jail apart and string up your stinkin' carcass to one of them beams."

Faulkner ignored him. His first act on entering the roomy office was to unlock a cabinet containing an assortment of weapons and take out a twelve-gauge shotgun. Several inches had been sawed from the barrels. Faulkner opened a drawer, extracted shells from a box and loaded the weapon purposefully. He propped the gun against the wall by his desk.

"There's your answer, Crudd," he said. "I'm through takin' orders from Fadden. I represent the law here, and it's about time Fadden and a few others realized I ain't nobody's hound dawg, not any more. Ain't nobody gettin' you out of jail. I'm holdin' the whole bunch of you for the circuit judge."

Crudd guffawed. He sneered, then spat to express his contempt.

"You're a damn fool, Faulkner," he growled, "all wind and red eye. You'll be buzzard bait before sundown, along with this here two-bit gunslick. And I'll—"

"Quit blowin' off steam, Abe," Newt Bailey protested. "When do we get something to eat, Faulkner? You aimin' to starve us to death? And this arm's givin' me hell. I want to see the sawbones."

"You'll get breakfast presently," the marshal told him curtly. "Leastways, them as keeps their mouths shut will. I ain't minded to take any more slaver from you hawgs. Doc Haggerty will be in later."

Shack Bonnatree grinned sardonically.

"Seems the marshal's got sand in his craw all of a sudden," he jeered. "You're pilin' up a heap of grief, old man."

"Fadden'll let the sass outta him sharp enough," Crudd declared. "If he don't I will, by grab!"

Loder approached the bars.

"Six months from now you'll still be cooling your heels in jail, Crudd," he warned. "And if you make trouble, I'll see to it that the judge tacks on another six months. Burl Fadden's through in Twin Rivers. The sooner you hombres realize that, the better. The law will have taken care of him, and *El Diablo*, long before any of you jaspers get out. Rope law, Crudd, or gun law."

Crudd made a grab at him through the bars, and swore when Loder neatly trapped the thick wrist and arm painfully against the metal. Cursing, Crudd jerked back. Loder followed the marshal into the office. Big John sat behind his desk. He was clean-shaven for the first time in weeks, and there was resolution in his expression, alertness in his eyes.

"You should have busted his arm," he growled. "What's the first move, Reed? You got a definite plan?"

Loder sat on the edge of the littered desk. He shook his head.

"Ain't much I can do except nose around and try to force Fadden's hand," he answered. "I didn't come here gunning for Fadden. But I reckon he's the key to the sidewinder I'm after. I intend to impose some regulations calculated to stir up some action, mebbe needle Fadden into making a wrong move. Then I'll close him up. If I keep pushing, sooner or later he's going to contact *El Diablo*, providing he is in cahoots with the snake. When he does, if he does, I intend to be right behind him."

"By now *El Diablo* will have gotten word you're gunnin' for him," Faulkner reminded him. "Could be he'll come lookin' for you and save you the trouble of smokin' him out. He's a right mean hombre, Reed. It ain't just him you're up ag'in'. There's thirty or forty greasers and half-breeds ridin' for him. You've bitten off some chaw, boy."

"I'll play the cards as they fall."

Loder found some stiff cardboard and spent the next few minutes printing a notice which he took outside and tacked to the weathered notice board. The sign read:

"THE WEARING OF SIX-GUNS WITHIN THE TOWN LIMITS IS HENCEFORTH PROHIBITED. OFFENDERS WILL BE JAILED FOR 28 DAYS WITHOUT THE OPTION OF A FINE. CHECK YOUR GUNS AT THE MARSHAL'S OFFICE. PICK THEM UP WHEN YOU LEAVE TOWN."

Satisfied with his handiwork, Loder nodded. He was about to re-enter the jail building when three men moved out from the shadows across the street and approached him, sauntering confidently. Two were tall, rangy hombres, the third short but very broad and thick-set. More of Fadden's men, Loder knew instinctively. The unkempt trio bore the unmistakable brand of the professional gunslammer. Their clothing was similar, drab and crumpled. There was nothing spectacular about any of them, but their common calling was obvious.

Rhone Vestry, the short man, wore a black shirt and pants. A wide-brimmed brown hat shaded his bleak eyes and shadowed his features, emphasizing his huge nose and prominent cheek-bones. A bone-handled Colt forty-four snugged into leather slick with oil slapped along his meaty hip. One of the taller men wore a fringed buckskin coat and brown leather pants tucked into knee-high boots with supple deerskin uppers and thick, hobnailed soles. A high-crowned black Stetson made him seem even taller. A sneer curled his thin, bloodless lips. Cole Tehaner's disposition was as ugly as his evilly scowling face. A drooping moustache conealed the corners of his mouth. His angular jaws champed noisily on a wad of tobacco. Brown spittle, escaping from between his foul teeth, dribbled down his chin. He wiped it away on the back of a bony hand. Tehaner packed two guns, slung low, the holsters thonged down. An arrogant, quick-

tempered hombre, Tehaner was one of Burl Fadden's
most useful hirelings, ruthess, fast with a gun and
afraid of no man. When it suited Fadden's purpose to
drive the settlers from the valley, Tehaner had led his
evil crew who burned the homesteads, ran off stock,
and shot down any of the sodbusters who resisted.
Since then, *El Diablo* had kept nesters out of the
territory in return for information that Fadden was in
a position to supply.

The other man, Frank Doolin, was one of two
notorious brothers wanted in four states for rustling
and murder. Cort Doolin had stretched rope some
months ago. Frank carried posse lead in his hip and
walked with a pronounced limp. He favored a
Peacemaker Colt forty-five holstered under his left
arm and carried a derringer hidden in the crown of his
straight-brimmed hat. His long black coat hung open.
A yellow bandana provided a splash of faded color at
his sinewy throat. A stogie hung from his bluish lips.
His eyes, close-set and mean, were narrowed against
the upward drift of smoke.

Loder turned slowly. Only a slight tightening of his
facial muscles betrayed his tension. A few yards away,
the trio halted. They spread out as if at a prearranged
signal. Cole Tehaner moved forward, smirking in-
solently, thumbs hooked into his sagging shell belt. He
peered at the notice with exaggerated intensity. Slowly

he spelled out the words.

"What d'you know, boys?" he crowed. "No totin' shootin' irons in town, it says. Seems we pore hombres ain't to be trusted with dangerous weapons no more. Haw! You aimin' to enforce this here notice, Loder?"

"That's the general idea, mister. Starting right now. You've read it. Shuck them guns and there'll be no trouble. There's pegs yonder in the entry to hang your belts on."

"No trouble, the man says." Tehaner spat contemptuously. "I've got news for you, gunslinger. Most hombres in this town can't read. Right, boys?"

His expression hardened. His lean body stiffened in tense anticipation. Hunched forward, with long fingers splayed above his holsters, he puckered his lips and deliberately directed a stream of spittle at the notice board.

"Like I said, Marshal," he gritted, "some of us don't read so good."

"So take off the guns anyway, fella. Or spend the next month in jail."

Tehaner wiped saliva from his mouth.

"Suppose you make me," he mouthed. Loder shrugged. Like a darting snake his fist shot out, smashed Tehaner in the mouth and hurled him against the hitching-rail. Simultaneously, Frank Doolin went for his under-arm gun. His fingers were closing round the butt when a bullet from Loder's weapon punched a dark hole between Doolin's glaring eyes and took away the back of his head in a welter of spattering blood, bone and mangled brains.

Tehaner, recovering more quickly than Loder expected, drew both guns with a smooth, whispering motion as he twisted away from the rail. But Loder had the edge. The weapon in his fist bucked against his palm, and blasted twice more. Both shots struck Tehaner in the chest and spun him round, jerking his bony frame. His guns fired harmlessly into the ground. Mouth gaping, eyes bulging, he fell against the rail again. It splintered, dropping his collapsing bulk to the boardwalk. Death stilled his twitching limbs in the same instant that Loder put a third bullet into him.

Rhone Vestry, confused by the incredible suddenness of Loder's reaction, mouthed oaths as he wiped his gun from leather and whirled, the hammer rocking back under the drag of his thumb. Fast though he was, Loder, concentrating on stopping Tehaner, couldn't have beaten the drop of Vestry's gun hammer. But an instant before Vestry got off a shot, the thunderous blast from a shotgun echoed from the jailhouse entry, and buckshot showered dirt and stones over Vestry's boots.

"Hold it, you varmint!" Big John Faulkner's

rasping voice warned. "I'll empty the other barrel plumb into your belly, Vestry, 'less you drop that iron, pronto! You all right, Reed?"

Loder nodded. He spun his gun, leathered it adroitly.

"Get inside," Faulkner ordered, prodding Vestry with the stubby shotgun barrels. "You there, young Rube, go get Doc Haggerty. Never mind, kid—here he comes now. Move, Vestry."

"Quit hazin' me, damn you! You won't get away with this, Faulkner. Fadden will have your hide for—"

The marshal shoved him impatiently. Cursing, Vestry climbed the jailhouse steps. Doc Haggerty pushed through the gathering crowd.

"Hold on!" he called. "What's been going on, John?"

"Reed Loder just filled another straight, Doc," Faulkner explained jubilantly. "Two more of Fadden's buzzards outa the game. Me and Loder aim to clean up this town, Doc. We can sure use some help. Pass the word around."

The medico stared.

"What's gotten into you, John?" he demanded. "I ain't seen you like this for a long time. Too long, by thunder! And sober, to boot."

"And sober I aim to stay, Doc. I'm doin' what I should have done a long time ago. Take care of things here. If anybody wants me, I'll be in my office. You men, them of you as can read, see what that notice says. Any hombre caught packin' a gun in Twin Rivers goes to jail for twenty-eight days. And that goes for everybody."

He followed Loder inside, leaving Haggerty gaping blankly. From across the street, Burl Fadden watched from an upstairs window. He swore vehemently. Fadden had seen the whole incident. Indeed, he had provoked it, fully expecting Loder to be gunned down by one or the other of the three gunmen. And but for Big John Faulkner, Loder would have been a candidate for Boothill. Fadden wasn't concerned about Doolin and Tehaner. The failure of his plan caused him to clench his fists. Anger put a flush of flaming color into his swarthy cheeks. He glanced toward the rifle leaning against the wall, a weapon he had placed there earlier, intending to clean it. He sent it clattering across the floor with a savage sweep of his foot. If he'd thought to pick it up and load it while Loder was still on the street, he could have finished what Tehaner and Doolin had started. Now they were both dead, and Rhone Vestry was in jail. Fadden glowered at Kate Molloy.

"I told you," she said, "Reed Loder's a hard man to kill, Burl. He'll stop the best you can send against him. You're—"

97

"Shut up, damn you! If that fool, Faulkner, hadn't horned in, Loder would be lying there with a hole in his head. But I'll get Faulkner for this. And you—I thought you were going to fix things with Loder. I was a fool to listen to you. Dad-burn it! I've never seen anything like it. Never would have believed anybody could down Tehaner if I hadn't seen it with my own eyes."

"Loder's dangerous," Kate agreed. "I didn't realize just how dangerous."

"You should have let Croft kill him when he had the long snake dead to rights. I'm a bigger fool for listening to you. With that big herd shoving up from the Rio Grande, and that gold shipment about due, this is no time to be playing around with a damn lawman. *El Diablo* is relying on us to deliver. We can't afford to let Loder get in the way. I never thought he'd take this marshal business so serious. You said he could be bought."

"All right, so I was wrong. What are we going to do about it?"

"I know what I'm going to do. You stay out of it. You had your chance. Now I'll take care of it, my way."

"Seems to me you already tried, three times."

"And who messed things up the first time?"

"Don't rub it in, Burl. You're no gunslinger. Reed

Loder will kill you just like he did Tehaner if you—"

"You think I'm loco? I ain't about to try my hand against that sidewinder. But I know where I can get hold of a couple of salty hombres who'll take him. Either one of them is plumb poison, more than a match for Loder, fast as he is."

"Wouldn't it be simpler just to shoot him in the back?" Kate asked, sneering. "It never bothered you before. Paul Teirney, for instance."

Fadden scowled. There were times when Kate got on his nerves.

"Sometimes you talk too much," he warned. "I could name you a dozen men who tried to bushwhack Reed Loder and wound up on Boothill. I never met him till now, but I've heard enough about the snake. I aim to make damn sure this time."

He laughed cynically.

"You've changed your tune all of a sudden," he accused her, begging for his life one minute, and suggesting I shoot him in the back the next."

"I don't mind admitting I've got a soft spot for Reed Loder. But there's too much at stake to allow sentiment to override common sense. He's bucking impossible odds. So far he's just groping in the dark, needling you. But why would he bother, unless he suspects? It's *El Diablo* he's after. So why not let *El Diablo* handle Loder? One word from me and he'll be here with twenty of his lobo crew. It's that fool, Faulkner, we need to do something about. If we let him get away with it, he'll have half the town backing him up before long."

"I'll take care of Faulkner and Loder. I don't want *El Diablo* thinking I can't handle one man, even a hellion like Loder. Get word to that cousin of yours, Karl. Tell him we expect Miguel tonight, and to let us know about the gold the moment he gets word over the telegraph. Mason will tip us off when the herd crosses the flats. *El Diablo* and his bunch won't have any trouble taking the gold off that stage. But he'll need every rider he's got to tackle that Brazos-W crew. Tell him my boys'll be standing by if he needs them."

"What's left of them," Kate jibed. "When are you going to do something about Crudd and the others?"

"In my own good time. Let the fools sweat it out. Time enough for that after I get Loder out of the way. I wish I knew if he was really playing a lone hand, or if he's got a Ranger troop staked out in the hills, waiting to crack down. He's too damned confident for my liking. I'll get word to Conroy and—"

"Linus Conroy? That cold-blooded snake?"

"The same. He'll cut Loder down to size. Meanwhile, tell the boys to stay out of Loder's way."

"All right. But why not spring Crudd and the others now, before folks get the idea Loder has you buffaloed? Surely there's enough muscle among our—"

"Forget it. We've lost enough men already. Besides, ain't none of the boys keen to buck Loder, and I don't blame them. He could blast them off the street from the jailhouse yonder, cut them to pieces with buckshot at close range. No, Kate. Leave Loder to me. Let me know when Miguel shows up. I'll be downstairs."

He went out, slammed the door behind him and descended the stairs. Across the street, Reed Loder unlocked the door of the cell occupied by Crudd and the rest of Fadden's men and thrust Vestry inside.

"Company for you," he told the scowling occupants. Ignoring their profane abuse and angry questions, he went through into the main building and closed the connecting door.

"The next move is up to Fadden," he told Faulkner. "I've a hunch if I play my cards right, he'll lead me to *El Diablo*. Right now I could use a thick, juicy steak with all the trimmings."

"Doan McGraw serves the best chow in town. His place is just along the street. Seems to me we'd best stay close to the jail tonight, Reed. But I reckon we can take time out to eat. I'm plumb famished. Y'know, Reed, I feel a lot easier in my mind already, better all round than I've been for months. This is the first time I've been really hungry in a coon's age. Let's go."

# CHAPTER SIX

Shadows were lengthening when Reed Loder followed Big John Faulkner from the jail and stood beside him on the wide boardwalk. The town was quiet, too quiet, Loder thought. The gunning of Doolin and Tehaner had produced the results he'd expected. All evening incoming riders had been checking their guns at the marshal's office, complying with the notice. It was all going smoothly, but Loder was apprehensive. It was like the ominous calm before a storm.

He struck a match and cupped flame to the stogie between his teeth.

"Let's make the rounds, Marshal," he said. He stepped into the street, pausing when he felt Faulkner's urgent grasp on his arm. Big John was watching the slow approach of a rider along the quiet main drag. The man, a fat Mexican swathed in a serape and wearing an enormous sombrero, tipped forward, hiding his face, rode past without raising his head and dismounted outside The Border Queen. He tied the dappled grey mare he'd been forking to the rail. As he ducked under the pole, his sombrero fell off. Faulkner swore. His grip on Loder's arm tightened.

"I know that greasy, black-haired skunk," he muttered. "One of *El Diablo*'s bunch. Name's Miguel Pasquale. I've got a reward dodger on him somewhere in the office."

"Nothing significant in that as I see it. From what I hear, that *El Diablo* sidewinder's bunch come and go as they please."

"Sure they do," Faulkner agreed, "more to my shame. But they don't usually sneak in by the side entrance the way that varmint's doin'."

Loder watched the Mexican move furtively along the side street to the narrow closed door, glance round several times before opening it and going inside. Presently a light came on, gleaming behind a curtained window.

"That's Burl Fadden's downstairs office," Faulkner said. "He's gotten a more elaborate layout upstairs. I always knew there was a close tie-up between Fadden and *El Diablo*."

"So I heard. That's why I'm here. Stay put. I'm going to see what I can pick up."

103

Loder crossed the street, keeping to the shadows, and moved quickly toward the lighted window. The streets were almost deserted. Lights were springing up here and there. Somewhere a dog was barking furiously. Loder paused in the lee of the saloon wall. The alley was shrouded in gloom. He tried to find a gap in the curtains. Unsuccessful, he pressed his ear against the grimy glass. Muffled voices reached him. One of the panes was cracked, and a small piece was missing. Loder applied his ear to the hole and listened intently. Fadden was talking. Occasionally Loder heard Kate Molloy interrupt. The Mexican, speaking in broken English punctuated by outbursts of torrid Spanish, was emphasizing the fact that *El Diablo* was becoming restless concerning a gold shipment. But the main topic seemed to be centered around a large herd of prime beeves being driven north from the Rio Grande. Kate Molloy's cousin, Karl Rennett, was, Loder gathered, to notify her when, and by which route, the gold was to be transported. Somebody named Mason would let Fadden know when the herd bedded down for the night near the Pecos River not far from Twin Rivers. Fadden's men were to join the wild bunch at the river. The whole gang would hit the Brazos-W drovers soon after daybreak, drygulch the night riders and sleeping punchers, and rustle the entire four thousand head.

# A BADGE AND A GUN

Loder remembered the brand name, Brazos-W. It was one of the biggest outfits in Texas. There would be upwards of thirty riders with the herd, all rangy, fast-shooting Texans. *El Diablo* must feel very confident of being able to pull off an ambush, Loder thought. And Fadden was to supply the vital information that would send the Brazos-W punchers to their deaths. Loder's expression hardened as he listened. Fadden and the Mexican renegade were planning wholesale murder, and Kate Molloy was a party to it. Her connection with *El Diablo*, and Fadden's, were proved beyond question.

Hearing his name mentioned, Loder pressed closer against the pane. A humorless grin creased his rugged visage. *El Diablo* had already heard of the gun-fighter's intention to bring the outlaw's vicious reign to an end, and *El Diablo* was not amused. He proposed, according to Miguel Pasquale, to silence Loder's brag personally, just as Loder had anticipated. The renegade's ego demanded that he deal with Loder himself. When the gold was in his hands and the herd safely across the border, then *El Diablo* would ride into Twin Rivers to nail Reed Loder's hide to the fence.

"We don't aim to wait that long," Loder heard Fadden say angrily. "That stinking gunslammer's already disorganized the whole set-up, started folks thinking, stirred up more trouble than you'd think any man could manage on his lonesome. Tell *El Diablo* I'm taking care of Loder myself, pronto."

Loder overheard some mention of Rangers and a torrent of abuse directed against lawmen in general. He had heard enough to formulate a plan, and moved away from the window and returned to the jailhouse.

"Learn anythin'?" Faulkner asked. Loder nodded.

"Plenty," he said. "Enough to decide what move to make. When that hombre leaves I aim to follow him. There's a plan afoot to wide-loop a big herd moving up from Texas. Heard something about a gold shipment, too. Hombre named Karl Rennett is tipping off Kate Molloy and Fadden about the gold. You know him?"

"Rennett? Sure, he's Kate's cousin. Operates the telegraph."

"That figures. Get inside—the greaser's heading this way now. Think you can hold things down here?"

"Durned right I can. By Gawd, Reed, this is almost like old times."

"You're doing all right, John. I've a hunch things'll work out. You say Ruth invited me for a meal tomorrow?"

"Sure did. She likes you, Reed. Always did when you were kids. She tries to hide it, but she can't fool me. She said to make it tonight, but I reckoned you'd want to stay in town."

Loder nodded absently. He had planned to spend the night in the jailhouse. He had been thinking a lot about Ruth Faulkner. Much of it was wishful thinking. But Loder had his hopes and dreams, like everybody else. Maybe, he thought, if he came out of it with a reasonably whole skin he could— He swore. Ruth had mellowed considerably, but she still thought of him as a killer, a gunslamming drifter steeped in the blood of his fellow men. And if anything happened to her father because of him— Loder shrugged. He dismissed the brooding notions from his mind as the fat Mexican approached the restless mare.

Miguel Pasquale was fat and filthy, but he had keen eyesight, remarkable hearing and the cunning of a fox. He knew that he was being followed even before he unhitched the grey mare. His expression didn't change perceptibly as he swung astride the creaking saddle. Only his beady, glittering eyes revealed his shrewd discovery. He kneed the mare to a fast run, and Reed Loder, riding from the livery stable moments later, held Satan to a steady canter and trailed the Mexican toward the brush.

When the dark growth concealed the man and his mount, Loder quickened the stallion's pace. There was, as yet, little moonlight. The gloom along the trail was intense when Loder entered the brush-flanked stretch. There was no sign of the Mexican, not a sound. Frowning, Loder reined in. The man couldn't have ridden so far ahead; he must be in hiding. Loder, realizing that he must have been seen or heard and his purpose interpreted, swore. He dismounted, drew his gun and stood listening intently.

Close by, dry brush crackled underfoot. He glimpsed a darker blur against the black undergrowth, but had no chance to shoot before a surging bulk smashed into him and bore him to the ground. The six-gun flipped from his hand. Knife steel glinted dully, striking at his throat. Desperately he grabbed, secured a grip on the Mexican's thick wrist and clung on. Fat though Pasquale was, he had plenty of muscle under the tallow, and bear-like strength in his gross body. Loder strove to keep the blade from his flesh and brought up his left fist in a punishing blow to Pasquale's flabby jaw. Miguel merely grunted. Loder hit him again, then drew his legs up, got one foot against the Mexican's gut and heaved mightily.

Cursing, Pasquale was hurled backwards. He landed among dense brush, rolled over and came up fast. But now Loder was ready for him. The pointed toe of the gunfighter's boot took the renegade under the chin and stopped him in his tracks. A savage right cross stabbed into his face. Loder followed up with a blow under the heart, hit Pasquale hard in the belly, then sent him sprawling with a vicious punch that connected with the man's temple. Before the Mexican recovered sufficiently to regain his feet, Loder located his gun and rammed the barrel against Pasquale's ribs.

"All right, renegade," Loder gritted. "On your feet."

He grabbed the front of Pasquale's ragged shirt and hauled him up. The gun hammer clicked sharply as Loder cocked it. Pasquale glowered, but there was fear, too, in his shifty eyes.

"What you want weeth me, gringo?" he demanded. "Who are you?"

"I think you know," Loder said. "But in case you are as stupid as you look, the name's Loder. Reed Loder, United States marshal. I want the answers to a few questions, Pasquale."

"*Caramba!* 'Ow you sabe my name? *Es todo un error.* (It is all a mistake). I theenk mebbe you are renegado, so I wait and—"

"Don't bother to lie, Mex. I *sabe* you're one of *El Diablo*'s bunch. I heard you talking to Fadden. Talk, you fat slob! Pronto—or I'll blow your damn head off!"

The gun shifted, pressed against Pasquale's forehead. He licked his lips nervously. He had heard many things about the gringo lobo named Loder.

Miguel Pasquale judged all men by his own depraved, immoral code. He would not have hesitated to kill a man in cold blood, and he believed that the gunfighter turned marshal wouldn't hesitate to carry out his threat, either.

"Wait!" he blurted. "*Por Dios!* I weel tell you what you weesh to know."

"*Bueno!* First thing—how far is it to the hide-out?"

"*Quien sabe?* Ten, mebbe twelve miles."

"It's in the badlands, near the border?"

"*Si, gringo.* Ees in the high sierras. But you weel never get—"

"Shut up! How d'you get into the place?"

Pasquale hesitated. The gun barrel ground wisps of greasy hair into his flesh.

"I'll ask you just once more," Loder threatened. Sweating, the Mexican nodded.

"There ees pass," he said quickly. "Only *un solo entrada*, no other way. Ees ver' *malo* trail."

"How many guards?"

"*Uno.* Only wan hombre."

"You're lying!"

"I swear it, on the grave of *mi madre. Madre de Dios!* Please, take away the gon. Eef the gringo's thumb should slip— I tell you the truth, senor."

Loder, satisfied that the man had given him the facts, lowered his weapon.

"Get your mare," he instructed. "We're taking a ride. Try anything, and I'll blast you out of the saddle."

Pasquale, quick to regain some of his composure once the immediate threat was removed, sneered contemptuously..

"*Si*, I weel take you," he agreed. "But eef you theenk to ride into the stronghold of *El Diablo* alone, you are either wan ver' loco hombre or—"

Loder spun him round and sent him stumbling toward the trail. Moonlight spread suddenly, silvering the brush. Pasquale, leading the mare, lurched into the open, muttering vindictively. He grasped the saddle-horn and prepared to mount. From a clump of trees, gun flame stabbed the night. The spiteful report from a rifle crashed sharply. Pasquale cried out. His gross bulk sagged, flopped into the brush. Loder, close behind the Mexican, shot twice toward the gun flash. A flurry of hasty movement was followed by another rifle shot, this time fired at Loder. But the bullet was deflected by the bushes. Loder shot again, but knew he had missed even before a drum of hoofs sounded along the trail.

He swore at his own folly. He had been too intent on trailing Pasquale to consider that somebody might be following *him*. He pouched his pistol. There was no point in chasing after the bushwhacker. Pasquale was

111

dead. Lodger sighed. At least he had determined the fact that the single approach to *El Diablo*'s hideout was guarded by only one man. If he could locate the pass and get into the place, perhaps he could finish the chore without the need to antagonize Fadden any further. It wasn't part of the deal for him to put Fadden out of business. His agreed job was to stop *El Diablo*. He had hoped that Pasquale would lead him to the outlaw camp. But he considered he could find it, and certainly *El Diablo* wouldn't be expecting him to make any such foolhardy move.

Loder dragged the body off the trail into the brush, then straddled Satan. He reloaded his gun as he rode. There were plenty of clouds, and the moon was repeatedly hidden, a factor in Loder's favor. Where the trail forked, one branch winding to the northeast, the other toward the arid terrain to the west, he followed the latter track and presently entered a bleak, desolate region of weathered basalt and broken buttes, wind-swept crags and lofty mesas. From the crest of a rise he studied the moonlit landscape, trying to form a conclusion as to where the renegade hideout was most likely to be amid that rugged desolation. He looked for smoke sign, but saw none.

He rode on, making wide sweeps to north and south and to the west. But he found no tracks, no break in the grim ramparts. He searched for hours, but was finally obliged to accept defeat. Disgustedly, he turned Satan's head toward town. It would need a large posse, he realized, to search the whole of that vast expanse thoroughly. Suddenly anxious about Big John Faulkner's welfare, he urged the stallion to a faster gait.

It was as the powerful black crested a steep slope that Loder heard the echo of distant gunshots. Reining in, he stared toward the low-lying ground fringing the badlands. Moonlight was again brightening the terrain, and he could distinguish the trail from San Antone winding like a long snake into the hills. A stagecoach appeared abruptly round a bend. It was being driven at reckless speed, jolting and lurching as the driver failed to avoid jutting rocks and other obstacles. An armed guard sat hunched forward beside the mule-skinner. He held a shotgun and was looking back anxiously over his left shoulder to where riders were swarming down the boulder-strewn slopes from the dense timber and brush. Loder tallied upwards of a dozen men and identified them as Mexicans, judging by their clothing.

Some of *El Diablo*'s bunch, he realized, remembering what he'd overheard about a gold shipment. Karl Rennett must have brought word soon after Loder left town, and Fadden had sent somebody else to notify *El Diablo*. Whoever Fadden had sent must have met the renegade at a pre-arranged rendezvous, and the gold was obviously aboard the coach. The raiders were using rifles as well as six-guns. Even as Loder reached back and hauled his Winchester from its scabbard, he saw the guard trigger the shotgun—a futile gesture—then fling his arms wide and pitch from the seat.

A thin smile curled Loder's lips. He was too far away for positive shooting, but he could at least give the driver a chance. He levered a shell into the breech, took swift aim and fired, shot again and again, and kept shooting as fast as he could operate the loading level and press the trigger. The slashing hail of slugs had a devastating effect on the bunched raiders. Three men spilled from their saddles. Shouts and curses arose. Lead ricocheted, whining ominously. Horses reared and plunged, snorting, wild-eyed. A fourth man was thrown to the ground when his saddle cinch broke and trampled by by thundering hoofs before he could roll aside.

The coach rattled on its way, the gaping driver plying his long whiplash and urging the sweating team to still greater efforts. Presently the vehicle lurched around another bend and was gone from view, and the rest of the raiders were hightailing for cover, shooting blindly up toward the ridge. Loder punched another man from the kak with a snap shot, then rammed his

114

rifle back into the boot and with grim satisfaction watched the outlaws retreating. Four down, five counting the trampled raider, wasn't a bad tally at that range. It was too bad about the guard. But at least he had steered the driver away from Boothill. Now *El Diablo* would really have something to get steamed up about. So would Fadden.

Loder kneed Satan to a fast run and headed the animal down toward the town trail.

# CHAPTER SEVEN

Meanwhile, back in Twin Rivers, Burl Fadden relaxed in a deep armchair in his downstairs office and studied the two men lounging near the closed door. They had ridden in soon after daybreak. One was tall and muscular, just a kid, not more than nineteen, with a shock of tow-colored hair that hung down over clear blue eyes as cold as frost. His face was like that of a much older man, deeply lined and cast in a hard, ruthless mould. An evil, arrogant face. His mouth was just a thin, bloodless gash. The Butane Kid was known throughout the southwest as one of the fastest gunslingers alive. His reputation was on a par with that of Billy the Kid or notorious Jim Ringo. A vicious, egotistical killer, a professional assassin, the Butane Kid gloried in his exploits. The twin pearl-handled fourty-fours slung low against his lean flanks in fancy hand-tooled holsters were for hire to the highest bidder.

116

# A BADGE AND A GUN

Jack Butane had many faults, and only one positive redeeming quality. He was true to his word, and he always paid his debts. There was, as yet, no price on his head, but like Reed Loder and other men who rode the dim trails, the Butane Kid was feeling the strain of being relentlessly hounded by bounty hunters bribed by his enemies, and by peace officers sworn to rid the Lone Star State of gunslinging desperadoes. He was young and resilient enough to shrug his broad shoulders and go his ornery way regardless, but even he was obliged to keep moving or use his guns against the law, to keep drifting, always one jump ahead of a bushwhack bullet or strangling, vigilante rope justice.

Yet even the swaggering Butane Kid cast a small shadow in comparison to the medium-built man leaning with his back against the door. Linus Conroy's sinister reputation was known and respected from the Rio Grande clear to the Black Hills of Dakota. Perhaps only once in a generation a man with Conroy's uncanny skill with a six-gun appears, a man so far ahead of other reputably fast gunslingers as to become almost a legendary figure. Linus Conroy was such a man. Short, of only average physique, he would have gone unnoticed in a crowd. Yet the carved bone grips of the single Colt forty-five he wore in a plain black holster was notched in more than a score of places, each nick representing the sudden demise of

117

yet another hombre brash enough to measure his gun swiftness against Conroy's. How many other men Conroy had left hopelessly crippled no man could say.

His hawk-like visage was an inscrutable mask, his eyes, iron-grey and rimmed with deep shadows, devoid of expression. Death rode in Linus Conroy's holster and in his long, supple fingers, in the gangling looseness of his sinewy arms. He was the best, and as such his services came high. The fact that Burl Fadden was willing to meet Conroy's price was an indication of the saloonkeeper's increasing desperation. Fadden leaned back in his chair, smiling confidently.

"Sure glad you boys could make it so soon," he said. "Take the weight off your feet. Have a smoke."

He gestured toward a silver box. Linus Conroy nodded, moved away from the door, reached out and selected a stogie. He bit the end off, lit the weed with a match struck on his gun butt, then resumed his casual stance. The Butane Kid darted a keen glance at the stocky killer. He ignored the box of cheroots.

"All right, Fadden," Conroy said. "I'm here. What's the score? And where does he fit into the deal? You figure I ain't capable of earnin' my fee without help from the Kid here?"

"Pull in your horns, Conroy," Butane told him curtly. "I didn't know Fadden had sent for you, too.

What's the idea, Fadden?"

"No offense, boys. It's just that I wanted the best, and you both came highly recommended. I wasn't sure if either of you was available at such short notice, so I sent for you both. No harm done. You'll both get your money, whichever of you downs Loder."

The Kid's eyes narrowed.

"Reed Loder?" he asked sharply. It was Conroy who looked up sharply this time.

"Reed Loder, huh?" he rasped. "I heard he was due to hang. Never met him, but they say he's purty good."

"Loder's plumb pizen," Butane declared. "I know him. He saved me from a lynch mob a while back. Sorry, Fadden. You've picked the wrong man. I won't pull a gun on Reed Loder."

"Suit yourself, Kid," Fadden said, shrugging. "I reckon Conroy here can handle it."

Conroy nodded. He regarded the Butane Kid calmly, sizing him up.

"My usual price for killing a man is five hundred bucks, Fadden," he said. "But Loder's kind of special. It'll cost you exactly double."

Fadden frowned and gnawed his lip.

"What is this?" he demanded. "You holding me up, Conroy? Just because the Kid wants no part of the deal is no reason to hold me up for double."

"Take it or leave it, Fadden. You hired two guns.

I'm willing to do the job on my lonesome. I'll take on the chore, at my price. The whole thousand, or I ride out. And let's get something else straight, Butane. Loder bein' a friend of yours, I wouldn't want you takin' cards in this game."

Butane eyed him coldly.

"Loder did me a good turn once," he answered. "But I reckon by holding off now, I'm repayin' the debt. I don't horn in on another hombre's contract, Conroy; leastways I never have. Loder's your huckleberry—if you can take him. They say you're faster'n greased lightnin', but I've seen Loder in action, and I wouldn't take no bets on who winds up on Boothill. But I'll say this, Conroy. If you take Loder you take him yourself, without anybody gettin' in a sneak shot like I heard happened over Ross Canyon way."

Conroy sucked in his breath sharply.

"You've got a big mouth, Kid," he accused. "Keep talkin' that way, and somebody's liable to put a plug in it."

"You, mebbe? Your reputation don't scare me none, Conroy. I've heard how you work. Any time you feel like shuttin' me up, I'll be pleased to accommodate you."

Conroy nodded. His expression didn't vary.

"I ain't no glory hunter, Butane," he replied calmly.

"I only pull my iron when there's profit in it for me. Unless, of course, some young punk was to draw on me, then I'd naturally have to kill him. If you crave action, Kid, you'll have to call the tune. But be ready to pay the piper. Me, I never mix business with pleasure."

"No call for harsh words, boys," Fadden said. He slid a full bottle across the desk. "Like the Kid says, Loder is sudden death. I want him stopped, and I don't care who does it, or how. I'll meet your price, Conroy. Half now, and the rest when the job's done. All right?"

"Suits me." Again the insignificant-looking gunhawk turned his chill stare on Jack Butane.

"There's nothin' here for you, Kid," he said. "Might be a good idea if you was to mosey on, if you get my meanin'. One thing more, Fadden. I hear Loder's packin' a U.S. marshal's badge. Don't make much sense, but it's reason enough for raisin' the ante, even discountin' the risks. It also means I can't afford to make the first move. Things have been tightenin' up a lot lately. It's gettin' so's a man can't hardly turn round without some lawman breathin' down his neck. And they're a different breed. Most of 'em can't be bought off, and killin' one of the badge-totin' buzzards only means there'll be two more along to take his place, and a rope waitin' at the end of it. Right now

the Rangers have gotten their hands full with Santa
Ana. But there's too many vigilante-minded hombres
hollerin' for rope reform to suit me. Loder's no
lawman. But he's wearin' a badge, so he's gotten the
law behind him. I'll have to make him come to me,
Fadden. That way nobody can say he wasn't pushin'
an old grudge and usin' the badge to cover up."

"Handle it any way you want. Just get him."

Fadden pounded his fist on the desk.

"I think I know how to bring Loder running," he
added. "There's a drunken bum named Faulkner
who's town marshal. Used to be purty salty, but now
he's just an old fool with a craving for whisky. Loder
knew him way back, and he's gotten Faulkner
believing he can whip the whole town again. Apart
from that, Faulkner's daughter blames Loder for
prodding the old man out of his rut. Loder's gotten
her talked round, and he's taken a shine to the gal. So
if somebody was to grab the marshal and hide him
some place, chances are Loder'll bust a gut trying to
find Faulkner, if only to keep in with the filly. It's
about time I peeled that stinking jail from off Crudd
and the others, anyway. Loder's out of town right now,
Gawd knows where, or what he's doing. He lit out
after—"

Fadden checked himself. There was no sense letting
Conroy and the Butane Kid know about the bush-

122

whacking of Miguel Pasquale or the reason for it.

"Time he shows up, we'll have things set up," he went on. "If you want to take a hand, Conroy, there'll be another hundred in it for you. The boys will jump around plumb sharp if you were giving the orders."

"Call your own dawgs to heel, Fadden," Conroy told him bluntly. "I'll handle my end when the time comes."

Big John Faulkner, seated behind the desk in his office, swung his booted feet to the floor and reached for the sawed-off shutgun when he heard furtive, scuffling noises outside the main entry and realized that somebody was out there. All night he had waited there for Loder to return, and he was half asleep. The temptation to drive brooding thoughts and doubts from his mind with whisky was demoralizingly strong, but he resisted it and swilled coffee instead.

His fingers were closing round the weapon when the door burst violently open and four men entered, surrounding him before he had a chance to use the gun. As he tried to bring it up a six-gun blasted. Lead tore a raw furrow across his side, and he cried out, dropping the shotgun. A heavy Colt barrel smashed down on his head, and he crumpled, with crimson staining his greying hair. Burl Fadden was with the intruders.

"Don't kill the fool," he cautioned. "We need

123

him."

One of the men with him snatched a bunch of keys from a peg and unlocked the connecting door. A tumult of profane excitement and raucous inquiries blared through the cell block when the prisoners realized the reason for the sudden commotion. Fadden himself released them. Newt Bailey's wounded arm had been bandaged, and he wore it in a sling. He darted to the marshal's desk and recovered his shell belt and gun from a drawer. Abe Crudd brutally drove his boot into the unconscious lawman's ribs.

"Bring him along," Fadden ordered. "I need him to bait a trap for Loder. After that, you can have him."

"What do we need a trap for?" Crudd growled. "There's enough of us to handle that two-bit four-flusher."

"You think so? So did Tehaner and Croft and Frank."

Crudd's bristly jaw hung slackly.

"He gunned Tehaner?" he blurted. "And Doolin?"

"And Croft, damn his eyes! But I've gotten somebody waiting in the saloon yonder who'll nail his ornery hide. It's costing me a thousand dollars. But it'll be worth it to get shut of Loder."

"A thousand! Who in tarnation—?"

"Linus Conroy, that's who. Sent for him and the Butane Kid both, but Butane quit cold on me soon as

124

he heard it was Loder I want out of the way. Wouldn't be surprised if Conroy didn't gun Butane, too, before he rides out. There ain't no love lost between them. Right now Conroy is waiting to call Loder's hand when he shows up, and I want to be there when Conroy kills the meddling son."

It was way after sunup when Reed Loder reached Twin Rivers and dismounted outside the jailhouse. Soon after starting back to town, Satan had planted a hoof in a treacherous gopher hole, and Loder had taken a nasty tumble that had laid him out cold until the early hours. No bones were broken, but he had a sore back and an aching head when he entered the gloomy building. He didn't recognize the buckboard he walked past. When he got inside, Ruth Faulkner was waiting for him, and she was almost frantic with worry. The cell block was empty, the connecting door wide open. The sawed-off shotgun lay in a corner, and there was blood on the floor boards.

The girl's face was pale, her eyes dark-ringed. Her grasp on Loder's arm was like a vise, her fingers digging deep the moment he crossed the threshold.

"Father!" she blurted. "He's gone! I've looked everywhere. And there's blood on the floor. Oh, God! I knew something like this would happen."

"Steady. Take it easy. We don't know what's happened."

"It's obvious what's happened. Fadden's men broke in and set Crudd and the others free. Father tried to stop them, and they shot him! They killed him, damn you!"

"Cut that out. Get a grip on yourself. You're jumping to conclusions. Could be that ain't his blood at all. Mebbe he left his mark on one of them. Look, if he was dead, why would they bother to remove the body? Fadden's trying some dirty game."

"Game?" Tears glistened in Ruth's tired eyes. Acting on a sudden impulse, Loder drew her close and kissed her on the mouth. She tensed, but didn't resist. He released her.

"Sorry," he said. "I'd no right to do that. You looked so helpless, so alone and miserable. No, damn it! I ain't sorry. Mebbe I should have done it before now. Gawd knows I've wanted to. We'll find your dad, and alive. How long have you been here? When did all this happen?"

"I don't know. I didn't arrive until a few minutes ago. I couldn't sleep all night for worrying. Finally I couldn't stand it any longer, so I drove the buckboard in. I thought you were with Father, Reed. You promised—"

"I was following a lead. Expected to be back hours ago. I had a fall—almost broke my neck. I'm still a mite shaken up. Have you seen Doc Haggerty?"

"I looked for him when I realized what had happened here. But I couldn't find him, either. Some of his friends haven't been seen since early last night. I don't know what's going on, only that there are a lot of strangers in town, gunfighters, Reed, some of them. I noticed two men in particular. They passed me on the trail, I could tell who—what they were. The signs were so plain. Nothing personal, Reed. But you do understand? I'm worried sick. We've got to find Father. Maybe, like you say, he is still alive."

"Of course he is. I'll find him. You get over to Doc Haggerty's place and wait there till he shows up. Don't argue. There's nothing you can do. Fadden's behind this. But he won't get away with it. I'll join you at Doc's place."

He was gone before she could think of anything else to say. She watched him striding rapidly, angling across the street toward the saloon.

From his leaning posture near the batwing doors, Newt Bailey observed Loder's brisk approach with mingled contempt and concern. There were no customers in the barroom. Shack Bonnatree stood at one end of the long counter, Abe Crudd at the other. Rhone Vestry and another man lounged on the upstairs landing, partly concealed behind thick drapes. In her room, Kate Molloy lay sleeping soundly, overcome by the drug which Fadden had administered to her in a cup of coffee the night before, his intention being to prevent any possible interference with his scheme to trap Reed Loder. He was taking no chances on Kate warning Loder or creating a scene. The laudanum would keep her quiet for most of the day, for Fadden hadn't spared the dosage.

Behind Fadden, close to the rear wall, Linus Conroy lurked in the shadows like a sinister, venomous reptile, hat tipped back, a stogie drooping from his sneering mouth. Fadden's expression betrayed his seething fury. Soon after he released Crudd and the others, word had reached him via Karl Rennett about the coach carrying the gold reaching its destination. Fadden couldn't understand why *El Diablo* had allowed the stage to elude him. He suspected Loder's hand in it somehow, although, as yet, he knew nothing about Loder shooting four of the renegade crew and frustrating the raid. The loss of his share of the gold was enough to put Fadden in a murderous humor, and his eyes glittered with sheer malevolence when Bailey reported that Loder was approaching.

"All right," he snapped. "You men know what to do."

"Let me do the talkin'," Conroy said, "and the shootin'. You hombres stay out of it."

Conroy knew Loder's reputation, but he felt supremely confident. The mere presence of Crudd and

the others was bound to rattle Loder, and that was all
Conroy needed to have a slight advantage. Not that he
really required it. He was the best, and he knew it. But
Conroy was familiar with every trick in the lethal
game, and he didn't miss a trick. He had an ace in the
hole calculated to infuriate Loder even more. As the
stocky gunman turned toward the batwings, his coat
swung open and revealed the silver star that Fadden
had ripped away from Big John Faulkner's shirt. It
was a supreme gesture of contempt, intended to
provoke Loder into drawing first so that Conroy could
prove self-defense if he had to.

Outside, on the boardwalk, Loder paused briefly
and eased his gun in the holster, checking its smooth
slide. He used his left hand to thrust the doors wide,
then entered warily, primed for swift action, knowing
that Fadden would be expecting him. He stopped just
beyond the entrance. Conroy's outline was indistinct.
It was Fadden, grinning mockingly, who confronted
Loder. The saloonkeeper was not wearing a gun.

"Wal, if it ain't the marshal," he jeered. "Looking
for something, Loder—or somebody?"

"Where's John Faulkner?" Loder asked. "If you've
harmed him, Fadden, I'll gut-shoot you, and you've
got my word for that. Where is he?"

"Suppose you ask the boys," Fadden mocked. "Or,
better still, the new town marshal. Speak your piece,

Conroy."

Hearing the name, Loder tensed. He looked round the room at Crudd and the others and knew he had walked into a trap. He wiped his suddenly moist palms down his pants. Conroy had never met Loder, but the Texan had seen Conroy a few times up around Deadwood. Conroy was sudden death, and Loder knew it. His expression hardened. The reason for Faulkner's disappearance was suddenly plain. He darted another glance at Fadden's men. Crudd and Bonnatree had their hands well away from their guns. Vestry leaned casually on the landing rail. The man with him hung back cautiously. Zack Dent was no hero.

Slowly Conroy revealed himself. A few rays of sunlight streaming over the distant crags shafted through a minute crack in the boards close to him and cast a crimson tinge across his unshaven jaw. He watched Loder closely. With slow deliberation he exposed the badge, rubbed his coat sleeve over it.

"So you're Reed Loder," he rasped, "the curly wolf I've been hearin' so much about. And packin' a star, too, by grab! Me, I ain't had mine long. Makes a man feel purty good, don't it? Kind of ten feet tall. Where'd you get yourn, big man?"

"Not from an old man too beat up to fight back," Loder answered coldly. His mouth felt suddenly very dry. Conroy alone was bad enough. But with Crudd and the rest to back his play— It looked like the end of the trail. Muscle ridged along Loder's jaw. He fought to curb his rising temper. The insulting retort wiped the sneer from Conroy's face.

"What have you done with Faulkner?" Loder repeated, speaking this time to Conroy.

"I ain't laid a hand on him," Conroy said truthfully, for he had taken no part in the jailbreak.

"You're a liar, Conroy!"

Only Conroy's eyes gave any indication that he had heard. Then he grinned, nodding to himself, knowing that he had it made. The added insult was the cue he had been waiting for. He took a step away from the alcove. His answer came, snapping like a whiplash.

"Prove it, gunslinger!"

What followed happened so quickly that Fadden saw only a fractional part of it. He glimpsed the blurring movement of hands driving gunwards, and realized with a surge of elation that Crudd and the others had followed his instructions and had ignored Conroy's demand that they stay out of it. Newt Bailey clawed out a gun with his left hand. On the landing, Vestry and Zack Dent both had their weapons clear of leather moments after the first shattering reports thundered deafeningly in the confined space. Abe Crudd was slower, though surprisingly fast for a man his size. Shack Bonnatree was throwing down even as Linus Conroy's thumb lifted from the hammer spur.

Loder's draw was the swiftest and smoothest he had ever made. But incredibly quick though he was, Conroy was a shade faster. His gun roared a fraction of a second before Loder's, the reports coming almost simultaneously. But a surge of vile, uncontrollable temper, caused by Fadden's men attempting to take the fight out of his hands, put a slight tremor in Conroy's hand. It was only a fleeting spasm, but enough to spoil his usually deadly aim, and the bullet intended for Loder's heart merely burned across his right forearm in the instant that his thumb lifted from his own gun hammer.

The searing lead burn wrung an oath from him. His arm jerked, deflecting his aim also, so that the slug barely broke the skin under Conroy's left arm before tearing into the wall behind him. Yet the brief, painful contact was sufficient to throw the stocky gunhawk off balance. And in that instant Loder switched the gun from his right hand to his left in a "border shift" too fast for the eye to follow and "fanned" the hammer spur five times.

The crashing detonations merged like one continuous report. Conroy, shot through the heart within an inch of the stolen badge, swayed like a storm-stricken tree in a high wind. Shack Bonnatree reared up onto his toes with blood spurting from a torn jugular vein. Lead tore into Newt Bailey's taut belly muscles, spun him round and slammed him against a table that collapsed under him, stabbing slivers into his sprawling corpse. On the landing, Rhone Vestry never even got off a shot before a slug took him between his staring, bloodshot eyes and hurled his body across the wide balcony. Zack Dent, caught in the act of leaning over the rail, died without ever knowing what killed him. His gangling bulk sagged forward, spilled slowly over the railing and plunged to the floor amid showering dust.

Loder's sixth and last shot scored a bloody groove along Abe Crudd's whiskery jaw as the huge longrider flung himself prone behind the end of the bar. He rolled over and shot twice at Loder from a kneeling position, missed both times and ducked back, not realizing, until Fadden mouthed venomous oaths, that Loder's gun was empty. He crouched there, glaring, fingering his bleeding chin, while the fact slowly penetrated his sluggish reasoning. He got to his feet then, savoring Loder's predicament.

The tall gunfighter stood straddle-legged with the smoking six-gun in his hand, waiting for Crudd to shoot again. But Crudd held his fire.

"Kill him!" Fadden shouted hoarsely. "What are you waiting for, you fool?"

Crudd took a step forward. The gun, rock steady, looked like a toy in his huge fist.

"He ain't goin' anywhere," he declared. "I want to see the stinkin' son sweat some more before I finish him."

He slouched toward Loder, lowered the gun barrel until it was aimed at Loder's stomach and stood grinning derisively. Loder, watching the hammer rocking back, felt a chill like icy fingers race up and down his spine.

The delay, brief though it was intended to be, was a fatal one—for Abe Crudd. A Colt blasted from the doorway, roared again. Crudd, shot twice in the chest, staggered back, open-mouthed. The gun fell from his slackened grasp as a third bullet whacked into his hairy torso and threw him against the bar. He toppled and pitched headlong, with arms flung wide.

The Butane Kid blew smoke from his ornate weapon. He pouched it deftly. His chill stare checked Fadden's furious outburst.

"I reckon that makes us even, Loder," Butane said. "Hell of a gunslinger you are, gettin' caught with an empty iron."

Loder turned. The relief he felt showed in his eyes. He forced a grin and began to reload his gun with sure, economical movements, locating shells in his belt loops by deft touch.

"It's been quite a spell, Jack," he drawled. "Don't mind saying I'm powerful glad you showed up when you did. How come? Don't try it, Fadden. You won't make it to the street."

Butane shrugged.

"Just driftin'," he said. "You sabe how it is."

"I reckon. But what brings you to this buzzard's roost?"

Butane jerked a thumb at Fadden.

"Wal, if you must know, Fadden here sent for me to gun you down," he admitted. "Didn't say who he wanted killed or I'd have saved myself the trip. I turned the job down. Conroy wasn't so particular. Never thought you'd cool him."

"I was lucky, Kid."

Loder lunged, grabbed the front of Fadden's coat and shoved him up against the bar.

"Mebbe now you'll tell me where you've got Faulkner hid," he rasped. "And if he's hurt, I'll crucify you, Fadden."

He balled a big fist and drove it into the saloonkeeper's stomach.

"Talk, you bastard!" he demanded. "Or must I beat it out of you? Believe me, it'll be a real pleasure."

Fadden's eyes bulged and watered. The breath left his lungs with an audible hissing sound. Loder drew back his fist. Fadden cringed and shook his head.

"In cellar," he wheezed. Loder spun him away from the bar and sent him stumbling toward the door connecting with the rear of the building. Fadden's face was convulsed with fury, but he offered no resistance.

Upstairs, Kate Molloy, only partly awakened from her drugged sleep despite all the shooting, thrust her languid body up from the luxurious bed and stared, bleary-eyed, toward the landing. Her eyelids felt as heavy as lead. Her mouth seemed to be lined with fur. She sat up, yawned and stretched like a great cat. The place was suddenly very quiet. Kate yawned again. Her eyes closed, and she fell back. Almost immediately she began to snore again.

Loder thrust Fadden ahead of him down the cellar steps. Jack Butane followed, prompted more by curiosity than interest. They found Big John Faulkner lying in a damp corner, securely bound and gagged. Apart from a bullet gash across his ribs and a bleeding scalp wound, he was intact.

"Thank Gawd you're all right," he blurted when Loder removed the filthy gag. "I knowed it was a trap. When I heard the shootin' I thought—"

"I'm all right. What happened?"

"Fadden and three other hombres jumped me. It all happened so fast I didn't get a chance to use the shotgun. They put a slug across my ribs; then one of 'em slugged me. They brung me here. Fadden allowed you'd come lookin' for me and had that Conroy sidewinder waitin' to gun you down."

"Conroy's dead," Loder told him. He helped the marshal to his feet and unfastened the clumsy knots. Faulkner raised his head and stared hard at Fadden. The moment he was free he made a sudden lunge and had the saloonkeeper by the throat.

"You dirty, no-good skunk!" he stormed. "I've taken all I'm goin' to from you. I'll bust your dad-blamed neck."

Loder restrained him with considerable difficulty. The marks made by the lawman's choking fingers showed prominently against Fadden's sallow flesh. Fadden massaged his bruised throat.

"I ought to let him squeeze the life out of your miserable carcass," Loder told him. "Get back up-stairs. I'm arresting you, Fadden. Move."

"You're loco! On what charge? Who the hell d'you—"

"Attempted murder. Assault on a peace officer. You name it. Move, damn you!"

Fadden started up the steps, scowling, but relieved to have gotten off so lightly. Loder had the whip hand for the time being, but he wouldn't keep it for long, once *El Diablo* and his bunch hit town. And when Loder was de-horned, Fadden resolved grimly, there'd be a reckoning. The screams out of Loder would be heard clear back to the Rio Grande.

# CHAPTER EIGHT

There was a commotion outside the saloon entrance. Ruth Faulkner pushed through the jostling crowd. Doc Haggerty was close behind her, as were several of the medico's friends, men who had once liked and respected Ruth's father. The girl thrust Jack Butane aside to reach Big John.

"Father!" she gasped. "Thank God you're safe. Reed Loder, you'll never know how very grateful I am, even though I blame you for what's happened. Maybe I shouldn't, but—"

"Beggin' your pardon, ma'am," Jack Butane butted in, "but that's twice you've tramped on my foot. Not that I'm complainin', you understand, you bein' so purty and all. But I sure would appreciate it if you was to ease up. Fact is, I've got about the worst dad-blamed corn in the whole territory."

Ruth ignored him. She held the doors open for her father. Loder turned abruptly and went back into the saloon. He bent over Conroy's corpse, plucked the star from the dead gunman's shirt front, straightened and shoved through the gaping crowd onto the street.

"Best get John over to my place," Doc Haggerty advised. "I'll look him over. Loder, some of the men are of a mind to call a meeting and appoint a vigilante committee to finish what you've started. Ten o'clock in the barn back of Jud Leary's feed store, if you're interested in saying a few words."

"I'll be there," Loder promised.

"Deal me in, too," Big John Faulkner said. "I'm all right, Doc. Damn it, Ben, it ain't more'n a bump and a scratch. You rustle up them as want to dicker, and me and Loder will tell 'em—"

"You're going to bed," the medico told him firmly. "I'll patch you up; then Ruth can drive you home."

"Like hell I'm goin' home."

"You'll do as Doc says," Ruth insisted. She seemed to notice Jack Butane for the first time and flushed.

"I'm sorry," she apologized, "for treading on your foot, and for ignoring you. I wasn't quite myself."

"Think nothin' of it, ma'am. I—"

"Ruth, please. Are you a friend of Reed Loder?"

"You might say we're purty well acquainted, ma'am, er, Ruth. Don't mind sayin' I'm mighty taken with you, Ruth. Purtiest gal in these parts, I'd say."

"Why, thank you, Mister—?"

"Jack Butane, though I'm mostly knowed as the Butane Kid. Loder saved my neck from a rope-hungry lynch mob a while back. I just repaid the debt."

"Crudd had me dead to rights," Loder explained. "Jack stopped him. Like you said, Kid, that makes us even, which same being so, I'll have to ask you to check them guns if you aim to stay in town, same as everybody else. I ain't playing any favorites."

Butane looked surprised. He shrugged.

"If you want my irons you'll have to take 'em, Loder," he said coldly. "How long d'you think I'd stay alive without 'em? That's a damn fool rulin' anyway, and it wasn't made for the likes of you and me. Right? You put up that notice to force Fadden's hand. Wal, you sure drawed his fangs, so you'd be smart to take it down ag'in."

Loder hesitated, then reached out and ripped the notice from the board.

"Mebbe you're right," he conceded. "If you are staying in town for a spell, Jack, I could sure use a deputy. You feel like tackling the job?"

"For reg'lar deputy's pay? I ain't stupid, Loder. It costs plenty to hire my irons."

"You'd be doing me a big favor," Ruth Faulkner said quickly, laying a hand on his arm. "I'd be most grateful."

Butane misread her meaning, and the appealing

expression on her strained, tense face. The Kid had left his mark on a lot of women, none of whom had been more than a passing fancy. But Ruth Faulkner was somehow different. She interested him strangely, affecting him in a way no other woman ever had. She had much the same effect on Reed Loder, but Butane didn't know that. He grinned. Ruth Faulkner wouldn't be hard to take, he thought. Fine-looking filly, a real thoroughbred, all fire and heart.

"Seein' as how you put it to me that way, I don't see how I can refuse," he answered. "Looks like you've gotten yourself a deputy, Loder. Purely on a temporary basis, you understand?"

Loder nodded. He held out the badge he had taken from Linus Conroy's body, but Butane shook his head.

"I'll pass up the tin star," he said. "I ain't no lawman, nor ever likely to be. No sense makin' a mockery of the chore. I'll back your play, Loder, for as long as it suits me, because this purty gal asked me so nice. But without the trimmin's."

Loder shrugged. He reached out and pinned the star on Big John Faulkner's torn shirt, then turned toward the jailhouse.

"You'll come over for a bite of breakfast, won't you?" the marshal asked.

"That include me?" Butane asked. Faulkner nodded. Ruth smiled approval, but frowned when

Loder said:

"Sorry, John, real sorry. I sure hate to pass up the meal and the company. But I've got things to attend to, and I don't aim to let Fadden out of my sight. Might make it for supper, though, providing—"

"You expectin' more trouble?" Faulkner demanded shrewdly.

"Just a hunch. I'll talk about it at the meeting. But there's nothing to keep you here right now, Jack. Go ahead. Ruth's a right good cook. You mosey back with her and John. I'll see you later."

Butane saw and interpreted the quick look of concern that flashed across the girl's face. He frowned. She was obviously worried about Loder. Butane shrugged. No need to rush things, he thought. Butter her up a bit first.

"Some other time," he drawled. "Seein' as how you talked me into takin' cards in this game, honey, I reckon the least I can do is stick with the marshal here. Shucks! Never thought I'd see the day when Reed Loder would be wearin' a tin star."

"All right," Ruth said. "Suppose we leave the invitation open? Fried chicken and blueberry pie."

"And all the whisky you can drink," Faulkner declared. "See here, Doc, there's nothin' wrong with me that Ruth can't tend to. Quit fussin' like an old hen and let me and the gal get along. Stop by later if you're so concerned. All I need right now is some rest."

"Well, if you say so, John. But—"

"I do say so. Hell! I recall the time I went three whole days with a couple of forty-four slugs in my carcass. Never quit the saddle. This ain't nothin', Doc. Let's go, Ruth. We'll look forward to seein' you boys. I'll be back in harness tomorrow, Reed."

"Sure thing," Loder agreed. "Take it easy, Ruth."

She nodded and plied the whip. Loder headed for the jail with the Butane Kid in step beside him. From the boardwalk they watched Ruth tool the rig along the rutted street and out of town. Jack Butane delved into his breast pocket for the makings.

"Durned if I ain't sore tempted to stick around for a while, Loder," he remarked, "just to make sure that gal appreciates what I'm doin' for her."

Loder nodded absently. He removed his hat and wiped his forehead.

"You hungry?" he asked. "I could do with a bite and a cup of coffee. Then after I've talked with Doc and his friends, I reckon I'll grab a few hours' shut-eye. Some time before daybreak tomorrow, the sidewinder they call *El Diablo* aims to run off a big herd moving up from the south. I intend to nail the buzzard; shouldn't be too difficult if I can rustle up enough help. Depends on how many men Doc

Haggerty can talk into backing me up. But I sure aim to try. Meanwhile, there ain't much we can do except keep our eyes peeled in case any of Fadden's crew still left in town decide to bust him out of jail."

"That ain't likely," Butane said confidently. "Let's go eat."

Shadows were lengthening when the Butane Kid shook Reed Loder roughly. Loder, lying on a bunk in Faulkner's office, opened his eyes, grunting a reply to Butane's gruff intimation that it was time he stirred.

"It's almost dark," Butane said. "You reckon we could ride out to the Faulkner place for a bite of supper?"

Loder swung his feet to the floor. He yawned, reaching for his boots.

"I'm staying close to town tonight," he said. "Had a long talk with Doc Haggerty and his friends. Seems they're taking this vigilante business plumb serious. Fifteen or more men turned up. From what I heard earlier, it appears the wild bunch will ride through here before sunup. We plan to give the snakes a surprise reception. Time enough for easy living when I get this deal tied up. But it ain't your affair, Jack, although I'll be powerful grateful for your help. Tonight's when I'll need somebody at my back. It's my guess somebody will try to get word to *El Diablo* soon as they find out about Doc's vigilantes."

"All right, so I'll stick around. You can burn in hell for all of me, Loder. I don't owe you a damn thing now. But I've taken a likin' to that gal, and I'll stay for her sake. First time I ever throwed in with the law, by Gawd! And for free. I must be gettin' soft. Let's go eat."

A clamor from the cell block sent Loder toward the connecting door, scowling. He knuckled sleep from his eyes, swung the door open and confronted Burl Fadden through the bars.

"Damn your stinkin' hide, Loder," Fadden complained. "You tryin' to starve me to death? I've been cooped up here all day without a bite, time you've been snoring like a hawg in there. You sure turned out to be a sour apple, Butane. I always heard you was a double-dealin' snake, and this proves it."

Butane leaned against the wall. He grinned wolfishly.

"Easy enough to shoot off your mouth when there's bars between you and me, Fadden," he said. "I didn't take your dinero, so what the hell are you complainin' about? You should have said who you were settin' up for Boothill before you sent for me. Fact is, I might just stay here, Fadden, the marshal's gal and me bein' kind of friendly, you might say. Even if the sawbones and his vigilante pards don't hang you, you're through in this town. Nothin' personal, you understand. But bein' interested in Faulkner's daughter, I'll just naturally have to gun you down first time I set eyes on you outside this here jail."

"I'll bring you something to eat," Loder promised. "Not that you deserve it, you low-down skunk. Meanwhile keep quiet, unless you hanker for a rap over the head with a gun barrel."

He and Butane withdrew. They went out, locking the street door behind them, and walked along to Doan Magraw's eating parlor. The moment he heard the outer door close, Fadden clambered up onto the cell bunk and resumed his gouging work with a large, rusty nail he had managed to pry from the bunk, chipping steadily at the adobe surrounding the single iron bar obstructing the small window aperture. Abe Crudd had considerably weakened the crumbling adobe when he was in the cell, and Fadden had been quick to notice the possible way to freedom. He had waited patiently for sundown, and his complaint about food had merely been a ruse to remind Loder and Butane of their own hunger and get them out of the jail building.

The bar was loose at the base. It required little further effort to dislodge it and expose the end of the rough metal. Fadden was a coward, but he was no weakling. Gripping the bar, he heaved, bracing his knees against the wall. The bar, old and flaky with rust, yielded. Fadden bent it inwards, then up, getting both his palms against it and thrusting repeatedly until the bar was well out of his way. Breathing heavily, he looked round the cell. There was a stool in one corner. Fadden got it, placed it on the bunk, and the additional height made it easy for him to thrust his head out of the window aperture.

The opening overlooked a quiet side street. There was nobody about. Quickly Fadden drew himself up and began to wriggle through the narrow gap. He wasn't a small man, and there was barely width enough for his shoulders. He lost a lot of skin in the process, but persevered, and eventually squeezed right through and let himself drop. It was only about eight feet, but he landed awkwardly, and swore with pain when his left ankle twisted sharply and his leg doubled up under him. He got to his feet, but found that he could use his left leg only with extreme difficulty. Agony stabbed his ankle every time he put any weight on it.

Fadden changed his mind about getting to the livery stable and started toward the rear of the saloon instead. The killing of Conroy and the others unnerved him. Hate twisted his face into a fiendish grimace. The Butane Kid would have cause to regret helping Loder, he resolved. The cheap, two-bit lobo whelp! But for Butane, Abe Crudd would have finished Loder. Now it was vital that Fadden get word to *El Diablo*. He had overheard enough, earlier, to know that there would be a blockade across the street with fifteen or more determined townsmen behind it, waiting to blast the raiders when they rode through Twin Rivers just before dawn. His grip on the town was gone, broken by one man. But the game wasn't played out yet.

Limping painfully, Fadden hobbled the length of the wall and turned the corner, hidden in dark shadows. He reached the rear of the saloon unseen and sneaked inside, groped through the gloom and opened the door giving access to the barroom. The place was deserted. Even the bartender was not in his usual spot. Loder, Fadden suspected, had put a lock on the batwing doors, and probably a notice stating that the saloon was closed.

Fadden didn't bother to find out. Acting on a sudden impulse, he limped to the bar and took the shotgun that the bartender kept under the counter, then turned toward the wide staircase and mounted the treads laboriously, gasping and cursing with every step. When he entered Kate Molloy's room, she was still sprawled out on the bed, awake, but lacking the will power to force her drugged body to get up. Fadden shook her roughly. Kate's head lolled. She muttered irritably, staring blankly at him.

"Snap out of it," Fadden gritted. "You've got some

riding to do. Come on, damn you! Move."

He dragged her to a sitting position. Kate pushed hair back from her eyes. Her eyelids drooped.

"What's going on?" she demanded. "What time is it?"

"Almost dark. You've been lying here since last night."

Kate frowned, trying to concentrate. She swung her feet to the floor, groaned and cradled her head in her hands. Suddenly the significance of his words penetrated the fog clouding her brain, and she raised her head and stared at him.

"Asleep?" she questioned. "All day? Till now? What are you saying, Burl? I'm all confused. What's been happening? I seem to remember there was shooting earlier, a lot earlier. Everything's hazy. What's been going on, for God's sake? Oh, my head!"

Fadden pulled her to her feet.

"Never mind your head," he snarled. "A ride in the night air will clear it. Get some clothes on."

Kate nodded dumbly. She groped across the room to a closet and opened the door.

"I don't understand," she complained. "Why would I sleep all those hours? I feel sick. I'm ill, Burl."

"I'll be damned! You had a headache last night," Fadden lied. "You took some laudanum. I warned you against the stuff. You must have overdone it. I've tried to waken you a dozen times earlier this morning, before Loder—"

"Loder? What about him? I don't remember anything about any laudanum, Burl. If I had a bad head last night, it's nothing to the head I've got now. It's splitting. Where am I going, anyway? And why? And what's Reed Loder got to do with it?"

"Get dressed and I'll tell you. And for Gawd'd sake, hurry! You're no sicker than me. There's hell to pay; everything's falling apart at the seams. Conroy's dead, and Crudd. So's Vestry and Bailey and—"

"Loder?"

"Who else? Damn his hellion soul. He ain't rightly human. Even Conroy couldn't drop him. Crudd would have if that swaggering fool, Butane, hadn't horned in."

Kate tugged on a riding skirt, fastened it and reached for a calico shirtwaist.

"The Butane Kid sided Loder?" she asked. "That's good. It was you who sent for Butane."

"How the hell did I know they knew each other? You know where I've been all day? Stinking in jail, that's where."

He explained briefly while she finished dressing. Kate, shrugging into a fringed buckskin coat, thrust her feet into supple, hand-tooled, calf-length boots, and stamped each foot a few times.

151

"I don't know where Ben is, or anybody else," Fadden finished. "Loder's got the whole town buffaloed. You've got to get word to *El Diablo*. He'll have to sort this out. Tell him what's going on, and about that fool, Haggerty, and his so-called vigilantes. He'll soon sort them out, by Gawd, after he runs that herd across the border. You ready?"

Kate nodded dumbly. She was still only half awake.

"Then get going. And watch out for Loder and Butane. I've got to rest this ankle for a spell; then I'll lie low. Loder doesn't know I've gotten out yet, but it won't be long before he finds out."

"What's the shotgun for? You've never been what I'd call a hero before, Burl. It's a bit late to be starting now."

"Maybe, but Loder ain't getting me back in a cell. I don't know why I bothered to send for Conroy. I could have done better myself—with this."

He patted the shotgun. Kate sneered. She picked up a quirt and whacked it against her leg.

"You're a low-down, sneaking skunk, Burl," she accused. "*You* administered that laudanum to keep me out of the way. You were afraid I might object to you bringing Linus Conroy and the Butane Kid here, so you drugged me. All right. At least I know where I stand. I'll go see *El Diablo*. But when I get back, we're through, you understand? Finished. I'll run my side of the business; you run yours. But anything else is out. All washed up, Burl."

She went out and slammed the door. Fadden heard her firm footsteps descending the stairs, then the slamming of the rear door. He swore. The amount of noise she was making, Loder would grab her before she even reached the livery stable. He stared out of the window. It was almost dark. His mind raced. It wasn't likely, he thought, that Loder would expect him to hide in the saloon. It was more probable that the Texan would think he'd make for the border. Perhaps the gunslinging hellbender was already aware of Fadden's escape and was watching the trail out of town, in which case Kate hadn't a hope of getting past him.

Fadden went through into his upstairs office. From the window he could see the jail entrance. There was no light in the building. Maybe Loder and Butane were still filling their bellies. Fadden sneered. He was ravenously hungry himself. But first he had to do something about his throbbing ankle. He limped to the washroom, ran cold water, soaked a cloth and bound the ankle tightly. The cold water helped. Getting his boot back on was painful, but he knew that if he didn't struggle into the boot, then he'd never get it on at all later on, and he might have to make tracks in a hurry if Loder came looking for him.

A disturbing thought struck him. Loder was no fool. Suppose he let Kate ride out and followed her to the hide-out? A grin replaced Fadden's scowl. So what if he did? Loder wouldn't stand a ghost of a chance of getting out of the renegade camp, even if he succeeded in getting in. *El Diablo's* men could smell a gringo a mile away. Fadden swore. What if Loder merely trailed Kate until he discovered the location of the hide-out, then returned and led Doc Haggerty's vigilantes into the badlands? Even the bunch of traders and sodbusters that Haggerty had rounded up could down a sizable number of the raiders if they managed to pull off a surprise attack.

Meanwhile, Reed Loder, with a liberal helping of steak and potatoes under his belt, washed down with plenty of hot, sweet coffee, followed Jack Butane from the eating-house and started back toward the jail. They crossed the street and stood for a while on the boardwalk outside the jail entrance, almost hidden in the shadows. At that moment, Burl Fadden was limping downstairs to the bar, intent on getting a bottle and killing some of the pain from his ankle with whisky. The gloom didn't confuse him. He found what he wanted, uncorked the bottle and drank from it, then started back upstairs. There was another way out of the cellar where he had kept Big John Faulkner a prisoner, a trap door giving access to the adjacent building, which Fadden also owned, and which backed onto the lumber yard he used as a "front" for various nefarious activities. He would, he decided, get some money from his desk drawer, then hole up in the cellar until *El Diablo* and his men showed up. Then if Loder came looking for him, he could sneak out and be long gone in the dark.

Down on the street, Jack Butane flipped his quirly stub into the dust and hitched up his gunbelt.

"Sure is quiet," he said. "If you ask me, the rest of Fadden's bunch have pulled out and left him to swing. Damned if I know why you bothered to bring that bag of cold vittles for him. A slug in the belly is all he'd get from me."

Loder nodded absently. He was staring toward the narrow turning flanking the livery stable. Butane shrugged, moved closer to the entry, but paused when Loder stepped quickly round the corner and stood hidden by the angle of the wall. A slow clatter of hoofs sounded. Presently a dark blob emerged from the deeper gloom—Kate Molloy, leading a pinto pony. She was about to mount when Loder strode forward and grasped the animal's bridle.

"Going somewhere?" he asked. Kate swore. She turned quickly.

"Reed! she blurted. "You startled me. I thought—"

"You thought I'd gone inside," he interrupted.

155

"Kind of late for you to be riding out of town, ain't it?"

"That's my business. Haven't you raised hell enough, you gunslinging devil?"

Her expression was vicious, her voice rough, embittered.

"Where I go is my business," she declared angrily. "Get away from me. I thought I knew you. I thought you had good sense. You think that gun is the answer to everything. I tried to reason with you, but you wouldn't have it. You had to prove how tough you are. I saved your life from Saul Morrow. And you repay me with nothing but trouble. You're kill-crazy, Reed Loder; just a cheap tinhorn. You've had a good run, but there'll be an end soon. You'll end up way out on a limb, and I'll spit on your carcass, Reed Loder."

She started to turn away, then grasped his arm impulsively.

"Oh, Reed," Butane heard her say, "why do you torture me? I ought to hate you. But I can't. Half The Border Queen is mine. When you hit at Burl Fadden, you hit at me, too. I ought to hate you. But— Why won't you see reason before it's too late? You're only human. You can't win. I'm offering you everything— money, power, influence, and my love. Isn't that enough? Damn you! What *do* you want?"

"*El Diablo*," he told her. "Dead or alive. I'm not

interested in anything else, leastways not right now."

Kate removed her hand from his arm as if his flesh had suddenly become red hot.

"All right," she snapped. "Have it your way. But the crows will be pecking out your eyes before sundown tomorrow."

She placed a foot in the stirrup and swung astride.

"Hold on!" Loder mouthed. "I ain't minded to let—"

Kate raised the quirt thonged to her wrist and lashed out spitefully. Loder flung his arm up instinctively to ward off the blow. The curling lash missed his face but coiled painfully round his forearm. Angrily, Kate whirled the pinto and rode into the night.

Jack Butane moved out into view. The moon was just rising above the distant mountains, beaming through hazy clouds. The Butane Kid was grinning.

"Some wildcat," he said. "You're a blamed fool, Loder. A man could do a lot worse than tie in with that filly. You lettin' her go, knowin' where she's headed?"

"That's why," Loder answered. "I'll give her a head start and then trail her. She might just lead me to that rattler's nest."

"And if she does, what then?"

Loder shrugged. Across the street, a dark figure showed briefly at a darkened upper window. Burl

Fadden, clutching the already depleted whisky bottle, sucked in his breath sharply when, having returned to his upstairs office, he saw the two men on the boardwalk and recognized them. Loder and Butane, together, less than fifty feet away. Hate convulsed Fadden's features. He put down the bottle and picked up the shotgun. Damn Loder, he thought savagely. Loder was fast, the most lethal gunslammer Fadden had ever encountered. But he was only a man, the same as Jack Butane, and they could bleed like anybody else. And Loder had been lucky, Fadden thought.

But now the gunfighter was down there in the street with his back toward the saloon window, and there was moonlight enough for even a novice to hit a mark at that range. Fadden was no gunman. But he felt a sudden surge of triumphant confidence that yielded to desperation and quivering fury when he saw Kate Molloy appear furtively from the alley and saw Loder duck back. Fadden rested the shotgun against the wall. Even Jack Butane, hawk-eyed though he usually was, failed to notice the slight, noiseless movement as Fadden slowly raised the bottom sash a few inches, then poked the shotgun barrels over the sill.

Fadden's lips writhed back from his gritted teeth. He had Loder dead to rights. The hammers were stiff under Fadden's impatient thumb. He couldn't miss, he told himself. Even so, his weak mouth trembled as he brought the weapon's scarred stock to his shoulder and completed the cocking movements. Yet, slight though the dull clicking sounds were, they were picked up by Loder's abnormally keen hearing. His reaction was instinctive and instantaneous. He went sideways in a sprawling lunge in the same instant that Fadden pressed both shotgun triggers simultaneously. The weapon's heavy roar boomed thunderously, echoing through. the building.

The lethal blast missed Loder's moving figure, but Jack Butane, less astute than the big Texan, was slower to act. He was just starting to turn when he received the full brunt of the double charge in the back and side. The force of it flung him across the boardwalk and draped him, torn and bleeding, across the jailhouse steps. Loder, gun in hand, rolled over quickly and came to his feet in deep shadow. He glimpsed vague movement at the upper saloon window and swore as he thumbed a brace of slugs towards the window. Glass shattered. But Fadden had withdrawn hurriedly.

The Butane Kid's eyes were closed, his mouth open, tongue protruding, dripping blood, bitten almost in half. It was incredible that the terrible injuries had not snuffed out his young life instantly. Cursing, Loder ran, ducking across the street, making for the saloon's

159

side entrance. As he went inside and up the rear staircase, Burl Fadden limped down the main flight. He was almost out of the street door when Loder came round the end of the bar and fired a warning shot that parted Fadden's dark hair.

"Drop it!" Loder ordered. "I don't need much of an excuse to kill you, Fadden."

Fadden released the shotgun as if it had suddenly changed into a rattlesnake. He raised his hands quickly.

"Don't shoot!" he blurted frantically. "Don't kill me, Loder!"

"You crawling scum!" Loder gritted. "I ought to—"

He took several swift strides toward Fadden, grasped the saloonkeeper's shoulder and spun him round. The barrel of Loder's gun lifted, slashed down savagely. Fadden, knocked cold, slumped without a sound. Loder leathered the forty-four. He bent, heaved the unconscious man up and got the dead weight over his shoulder. He kicked the batwings open and carried Fadden out and across the street to the jail, ignoring queries and clamoring comments. He unlocked the main door, went through the office, unlocked the connecting door, and dumped his burden roughly into the cell adjoining the one Fadden had escaped from earlier. He inspected the barred window briefly. Satisfied, he locked the cell door and

160

put the keys in his pocket, then went out, secured the jailhouse door and headed for the livery stable.

Minutes later he rode along the main drag to where Doc Haggerty, hampered by a jostling crowd, was keneeling beside Jack Butane.

"How is he, Doc?" Loder asked. The medico shook his head.

"It's bad," he said. "If he lasts for another ten minutes, it'll be a miracle. Some of you men help me get him across to my place. You ridin', Loder?"

"I'll be back before sunup. Have your bunch standing by, but don't do anything till I show up."

Haggerty nodded. He stood up.

"Who shot Butane?" he asked.

"Fadden. I had him in jail, but he broke out. That buckshot was intended for me. He's inside again, and this time he won't get out until he's taken out and tried for murder. I can't talk here, Doc. I'll see you later. Be ready."

He turned Satan and kneed the stallion to a fast run, heading for the badlands, intent on overtaking Kate Molloy.

# CHAPTER NINE

The clatter of hoofs crossing stony ground warned
Reed Loder that the rider ahead of him was moving
much slower. Loder had glimpsed the shadowy figure
often enough to know that it was Kate Molloy. He had
pushed Satan hard, and the powerful stallion had
responded nobly. Loder, grim-faced, was certain now
that his earlier suspicions were well-founded, that he
knew the secret identity of *El Diablo*. Fadden had
become sufficiently alarmed to send Kate hightailing
for the one man they thought could stop Loder—the
vicious renegade Loder was determined to get, dead or
alive. And the way Kate had reacted convinced Loder
that she and *El Diablo* were more than just partners in
a nefarious rustling and high-grading set-up.

Sure now that his hunch was right, Loder held
Satan to a mile-killing pace until he heard the
hoofbeats. He slowed the snorting animal then and
matched the gait of the pinto up ahead. The terrain

was becoming continually bleaker and more rugged. Treacherous shale shifted underfoot. Great boulders loomed against the night sky. Moonlight emphasized valleys and hollows, dangerous chasms and steep hogbacks. Obviously, Kate Molloy had ridden over that winding trail many times before. When Loder came across fresh dung steaming on the track, he reined the stallion to a walk. The rising trail was hemmed in by the sheer rock face on both sides. Ahead, the canyon narrowed until there was barely room for a horse to pass. Loder heard water splashing. Suddenly he heard voices, urgent, demanding—the voice of a man speaking in Spanish, then Kate Molloy's impatient answer. A grim smile curled Loder's lips. Kate had led him straight to the hide-out—to *El Diablo*.

He dismounted, left Satan hitched to a dead tree and continued on foot. He had already established, from Miguel Pasquale, that only one man guarded the pass. If he could dispose of the guard quietly, then the element of surprise would be in his favor. He moved forward, clambering swiftly but without noise over the weathered rocks, climbing all the time until he reached the bulge of a great rock overlooking a moonlit valley that stretched for miles. Against the northeast wall, almost hidden by tall trees, he saw several large shacks. The acrid tang of wood smoke reached his nostrils. There were a number of horses in a pole corral. Loder tallied about thirty animals. He frowned.

Long odds. Now that he had found the hide-out, supposing he did get past the guard, what then? He shrugged. If he got *El Diablo*, the rest wouldn't amount to shucks. With their leader dead, they'd probably hightail across the border. But he would have to play it cagey, lie low and wait for a chance to drop *El Diablo*, making sure he left himself an escape route open. He climbed higher, inched round a narrow ledge. Rocks hid the valley from view. Suddenly aware of vague movement, he stopped. A match flared. The smoke from a stogie drifted upwards. Loder's eyes narrowed. The guard was just below him, standing in the shadow cast by the boulder.

Loder drew his gun, quickly estimated the distance and jumped. His guess had been a good one. He landed within a foot of a hulking, raggedly dressed Mexican who sat on a rock staring vacantly after the departing pinto, then disappearing beyond waving manzanita brush. The man twisted round, mouth open to yell, eyes widening in surprise. He made a desperate effort to swing up the rifle lying across his knees. But he never had a chance. Loder's gun barrel smashed down.

The Mexican crumpled, flopped sideways and lay huddled. Loder picked up the rifle. He followed the pinto, moving cautiously. The faint sounds of hoofs had ceased, as if Kate Molloy were riding over grassy terrain. Carrying the rifle, Loder kept walking. Ahead, the narrow pass curved. The bend and beyond was steeped in darkness, until Loder, loping silently past a grotesque formation of huge boulders, reached a more open, exposed stretch where moon rays penetrated. Rounding the bend, Loder stopped abruptly. He swore. Several riders, mostly Mexicans, were bunched on the trail, completely blocking it. A dozen guns threatened Loder.

In the lead, Kate Molloy sat her pinto pony. Her expression was a combination of triumph and frowning concentration. Beside her, a tall, gangling white man, bearded, and wearing fringed buckskins, straddled a big roan gelding. His eyes were green, flecked with amber streaks like those of a cat. They reflected utter ruthlessness, a savage and evil disposition. His sneering mouth was just a thin, bloodless gash against a face puckered and criss-crossed with innumerable scars. Twin bone-handled Colt forty-fives weighted down a plain black shell belt nipping in his narrow waist. His hair, dark and greasy, hung down below the level of his sagging shoulders.

Reed Loder recognized the man even before *El Diablo* shoved back the cream-colored Stetson he wore and moonlight revealed his features.

"Hello, Kate," Loder said. "Seems you're smarter than I gave you credit for. I had a hunch *El Diablo* was your brother. Never did cotton to that yarn about you being butchered by Indians, Molloy."

*El Diablo*, alias Denton Molloy, grinned malevolently, exposing firm white teeth.

"So you're Loder," he said contemptuously, "the law-dawg with the big mouth. Gunslinger turned U.S. marshal, huh? You cheap tinhorn! I heard you was lookin' for me, Marshal, special commission and all. Wal, so now you've found me. It's a meetin' you're liable to regret, Loder."

He spat and motioned for Loder to drop the rifle.

"What are you waiting for?" Loder demanded, letting the weapon fall to the ground. "I won't deny I came here to kill you, Molloy."

"You stubborn fool!" Kate broke in bitterly. "Why didn't you listen to me? I told you how it would end. I warned you, gave you every chance. Now it's too late. I had a hunch you'd try to follow me. I wish you hadn't, Reed. Sanchez is a fool. I told him you would probably trail me here. Yet he let you sneak up on him. I watched you scale the rocks, Reed, expected Sanchez to be ready for you. I saw you club him. A lot of trouble, Reed, for nothing. Oh, why wouldn't you listen to me? I can't save you now."

Her outlaw brother tipped his hat further back.

"Ain't it the truth," he jeered, "although I don't mind admittin' I admire your nerve, Loder. Any hombre who can drop Linus Conroy must be purty good. But there's faster guns than Conroy's ever was, tinhorn. Mine, for instance. Best shuck your iron, Lawman. I ain't minded to kill you just yet, but don't try anythin' foolish. Pedro, get his gun."

A villainous-looking 'breed sitting a shaggy claybank mustang slightly behind *El Diablo*, bared broken teeth in a leering smirk.

"Why we not keel this gringo peeg now?" he demanded. "He geeve much tro'ble, this wan. I theenk mebbe ees the hombre who shoot *compadres* and allow the coach weeth the gold to get away. *Si*, he ees the man. *Caramba!* I weel cut out his—"

"*Alto!* I give the orders here, Vincente. Loder, I've heard plenty about you. That badge don't mean a damn thing—I *sabe* how the governor's gotten you over a barrel. Wal, I like a man who can handle himself, and I can use a smart hombre like you, gunslammer. Ain't nobody in these parts about to put a rope around your neck. Listen. Kate here thinks a heap of you; that's why I'm willin' to make a deal with you now. She tells me she's tried to persuade you to get your head out of the clouds and throw in with her, which is the same as throwin' in with me. I figure it's on account of you havin' to choose between that star and the rope that you turned her down. Wal, nobody says no to my sister, Loder. I've been losing some good men lately, one way or another. Mostly white men, by thunder! And the bunch I boss don't get along with gringos. But I reckon a tough hombre like you could keep the buzzards in line, same as I do."

His green eyes glittered. So quickly that Loder hardly saw the man's hand move, *El Diablo* drew a gun. The barrel lined up on Loder's forehead. The hammer snicked to full cock.

"You've been raisin' hell a-plenty in town," Molloy accused. "Got Fadden goin' round in circles, the damn fool. I ought to kill you right now. But for Kate's sake I'm goin' to give you a break, Loder, time to think it over before you decide. They tell me you're a man of your word. *Bueno!* So now I'm tellin' you, gunslinger. You either throw in with me and Kate and take what she's offerin'—or you get what's comin' to you, pronto. I'll give you a little time. Don't worry about Fadden's end of the deal. He's been on the way out for some time. Never did see what Kate found attractive in the yaller dawg. I like a jasper with guts, Loder, which is another reason why you're still breathin'. I've got a good thing goin' here, Loder. Throw in with me and I'll make you rich. Buck me, and you wind up dead. You've got until noon tomorrow to make up your mind. Right now I've got important business to take care of. Vincente, herd the gringo into the barn yonder and rope him good and tight. Tell Ortega to watch him. Let's ride, you hellions. You'd best stay here, Kate. And keep away from Loder."

"I'm through trying to make up his mind," Kate declared. "From now on he's on his own. I'm riding back to town, Denton. I'm more than a mite concerned about what Doc Haggerty's up to."

"Haggerty?"

"Yes. Didn't Ramone tell you? The sawbones has been getting some big ideas lately. He's been making vigilante talk ever since Loder gunned Conroy and a few of Fadden's men. And that fool, Faulkner, is rearing up on his hind legs, too; thinks he's still man enough to lick Twin Rivers back into the same shape the town used to be in. Reed, what was that shooting I heard just after I rode out? I'm sorry about lashing you with the quirt. But you make me so mad."

"Fadden shot Jack Butane in the back with a shotgun," Loder explained curtly. "I don't know how he got out of jail, but he's back in, and he'll stay there till they hang the low-down snake."

The outlaw, Pedro, pushed him roughly towards the shacks. *El Diablo* spat.

"Watch him," he ordered. "I'll take care of Faulkner, Kate. And Fadden. Burl knows too much.

I'll bust him out of jail all right, and then he'll happen to have a little 'accident.' I'm more interested in them steers right now. This'll be the biggest haul yet."

Kate nodded. She watched Vincente and Pedro and another man hustling Loder toward the barn.

"The herd is bedded down just a few miles south of town, Denton," she told her brother. "Maybe four thousand head."

"How many riders?"

"At least forty. It won't be easy. You'll have to hit them hard and fast."

"I ain't never lost a herd yet, sister. We'll go through town and—"

"No! Best avoid town. Burl overheard Loder and Butane talking. Doc Haggerty's raising a posse. I don't know how many men, but I figure they'll be waiting for you to ride through Twin Rivers. They may not amount to shucks without Loder to take charge. But they could cost you a few men and slow you down."

"All right. So we'll swing around and lie low till daybreak, then drift on to the herd out of the sun, whittle down the crew with rifle fire and hit the rest on the run. If we leave now we've no need to run our broncs into the ground gettin' to the river crossin'. We'll take care of the marshal and Haggerty's bunch on the way back, after the boys start the herd toward

170

the border. You stay at the saloon and keep out of
sight. If you can round up the rest of Fadden's men,
tell them to ride herd on Haggerty's fools. All right,
you rangy lobos. Let's ride."

Loder offered no resistance. Rough hands grasped
him, hurried him onward. Somebody opened the barn
door, and he stumbled over the threshold, over-
balanced by a violent push from behind. A fat, pock-
marked half-breed, Ortega, pressed the keen point of
a knife against the Texan's throat. Another man
uncoiled a lariat, dabbed the loop over Older's wrists
and drew it tight, then took several hitches round his
ankles, drawing his legs up tight and securing him in a
doubled-up position.

"That weel hold the *malo* gringo gonfighter,"
Vincente declared. "This hombre I do not trust, but
*El Diablo* geeve the orders here. Eef you decide to ride
weeth us, gringo, *bueno*! Here we all *amigos*. The life
of *el renegado* ees ver' good. But eef you are foolish,
*senor*, then—" He drew a finger suggestively across
his throat, then turned quickly and went out into the
moonlight, followed by all the rest except Ortega, who
stood in the doorway and watched the others ride after
the main bunch.

Reed Loder, lying stiff and cramped on foul-
smelling straw, swore as the rough hemp chafed his
flesh. He was, he knew, very lucky to be alive. But

171

unless he gave Denton Molloy his word and threw in with the outlaw, he would never leave the valley alive, and Loder had a strong suspicion that *El Diablo* had spared his life at the time only because Kate had been there and the renegade was strongly influenced by his sister. Maybe, once Kate was out of the way, Denton Molloy would have Loder killed, or would take a fiendish delight in killing the gunfighter-marshal himself. There was no mercy in Denton Molloy's black soul. The fact that Loder knew the outlaw's secret identity was more than enough to seal his fate.

Because of Kate's warning, the plan to throw up a barricade across the town's main street and ambush the raiders on their way through Twin Rivers was now useless. Molloy would circle the town before dawn and stake out his gang where they could shoot down the unsuspecting Brazos-W riders as they crouched, bleary-eyed and shivering, round the fire, or crowded round the chuck-wagon. Others of the outlaw crew would be waiting to gun down the night riders when Mollow gave the signal. It would be a bloody massacre.

Loder swelled his muscles, trying again to slacken the tough rope, but only broke the already raw skin. Ortega was outside, hunched on a bench with his broad back against the door and a rifle across his legs, head lolling, eyes closed. He had Loder's six-gun

172

thrust inside his belt. The barn was in darkness, the outlaw camp silent. Loder swore. Somehow he had to escape and warn the Brazos-W outfit. If he could pick up Doc Haggerty and the vigilantes on the way and reach the herd before *El Diablo* struck, there was still a chance to turn the tables on Denton Molloy.

Loder rolled over and came up against the wall. Straw rustled. A large rat scampered across the floor and darted into a cavity. Loder tried again to stretch the rope, but desisted when he realized the utter futility of trying to break the strands. Then his boot heel struck against something metallic. The sound promoted a faint ray of hope, and he kicked at the object, disturbing it under the straw. He couldn't see what it was, but groped about until his fingers touched rusty metal and traced a jagged rim. An empty can of some sort, he realized. He managed to pick it up, but dropped it when he attempted to twist round and bring the ragged edge against the lariat. After further effort he got the can again, and this time persevered until he was able to wedge it between two warped posts, part of the end of a stall. By lying on his side with his shoulder jammed against the boards, he was able to saw the rope against the sharp tin.

It was a slow, painful process, and he swore often as he lacerated his flesh. But eventually he felt some of the strands part, and when he exerted his strength the remainder yielded. The relief of being able to straighten his legs was acute. It didn't take him long to slash through the lariat binding his ankles. Finally he could stand. He chafed his sore, bleeding wrists, crept to the door and listened with his ear against it. Ortega was snoring. But he was seated with his bulk against the door, and there was no other way out. Loder groped round for a weapon, but found only pieces of the severed rope.

He delved into his coat pockets, found a match and struck it. The feeble flame revealed an assortment of litter, but there was no break in the wall, no opening or boarded-up window. He picked up a length of rusty chain, then deliberately dropped the burning match into a heap of straw. Smoke began to curl, dense and pungent. Loder waited until flames were licking up, then voiced a loud yell. The effect on Ortega was instantaneous. He jerked erect, banged his head against the boards and lurched to his feet. The rifle clattered to the ground. Rubbing his head and muttering, the fat Mexican banged on the door.

"*Silencio*, gringo!" he demanded. "What ees matter? You 'ave gone loco mebbe?"

"Fire!" Loder shouted. "The barn's on fire!"

Ortega swore. His dim mentality tried to grapple with the problem of how a fire could have started. Smoke began to issue from under the door.

"Open up!" Loder shouted. "Let me out of here. I'll be roasted alive!"

"*Por Dios!*" Ortega exclaimed. Renegade though he was, he didn't want the gringo's death by burning on his conscience. He dragged the bench aside and swung the door open. Acrid smoke billowed out. Through the haze he glimpsed blurred movement, and hesitated. In that instant Loder swung the heavy chain. The links struck Ortega above the left ear and dropped him in an inert heap. Loder bent, snatched his gun from the stunned outlaw's belt and ran toward the corral, dragged the gate open and picked up a lariat coiled on a post. Selecting a big roan, he roped the animal expertly. Moments later he was heading for the pass, riding bareback.

Behind him flames were rising swiftly, curling round the dry timbers. Unless Ortega woke up presently, he would be consumed by flames as hot as the hell-fire he was ultimately destined for. Loder hadn't thought to drag the man clear of the barn, and he had no time to go back. The lives of thirty or even forty men depended on him reaching the river crossing before the raiders struck. When he approached the entrance to the pass, the guard, Sanchez, was no longer lying on the ground. He had obviously recovered and had gone with *El Diablo* and the others. Loder rode from the valley and into the brush. Satan was munching grass contentedly where Loder had left him.

Within moments, Loder had switched mounts, and the stallion was thundering toward Twin Rivers.

# CHAPTER TEN

It was almost daybreak when Reed Loder rode into Twin Rivers. There was more activity than he had expected. The Border Queen was in darkness except for a faint glimmer from a front upper room, but lights gleamed here and there, and groups of men were gathered on the street. There was also a light in Big John Faulkner's office. Loder found the marshal at the jail. Ruth was with her father and Doc Haggerty.

"Thank Gawd you're all right, boy," Faulkner commented when Loder entered. "I couldn't rest for thinkin' what might be happenin' here. I had to come back. Ruth wouldn't stay home alone. When we l'arned as how Fadden done broke out of jail and shot young Butane, and we couldn't find hide nor hair of you, we was worried plumb sick. Where you been?"

"Hunting me a skunk in the badlands yonder. How is Butane, Doc?"

"Your friend is dead," Ruth said before the medico could reply. "That poor boy—for that's all he was, just a boy—never regained consciousness."

"Fadden'll hang for that," Loder promised. "There's no time for long-winded explanations. I trailed Kate Molloy to the gang's hide-out. The sidewinder they call *El Diablo* is her brother, Denton Molloy."

Faulkner gaped. He shoved his chair back.

"Denton Molloy!" he growled. "That murderin' buzzard? But I thought Molloy was dead, killed by Injuns. Kate always allowed as how—"

"She would, naturally. It ain't no ghost leading that bunch of greasers. Kate warned them there'd likely be men waiting in town to throw lead their way. They're riding wide of Twin Rivers."

"Word's gotten out about the vigilantes," Haggerty told him. "There ain't one of Fadden's men left in town. Kate rode in a while back, alone. She's up in her room above the saloon, as far as I know. There's talk of riding her outa town on a rail."

"She'll keep, I reckon. Molloy's bunch aim to drygulch the Brazos-W range crew and rustle the herd. I had a hunch that Kate Molloy had a closer connection with *El Diablo* than just a crooked business deal. She was too damned eager to steer me away from the sidewinder. That brother of hers is plumb poison. He's got to be stopped, and there'll never be a better chance than now. How many men d'you reckon you can rely on now that the chips are down, Doc?"

"A dozen, mebbe fourteen, leastways till the shootin' starts."

"All right. Round them up and start them for the river crossing. That's where *El Diablo* plans to hit the herd. You sit tight here, John. I'm riding for the Brazos-W pronto to warn them. Could be there's still time. Doc, you hold your men near that yellow bluff south of Old Baldy until you hear two shots close together. That'll be the signal to move in fast. We'll catch them buzzards in a crossfire. You stay with your father, Ruth. If things work out, I'll be taking you up on that supper invitation."

"I'm ridin' with Doc," Faulkner declared resolutely.

"Suit yourself," Loder told him. "Mebbe you'd best get over to Doc's place, Ruth. This ain't no place for you. Is Fadden still locked up back there, John?"

"Sure is, Reed. I've been expectin' another attempt to bust him out. But like Doc says, the rest of his bunch have hightailed."

"You'd best leave a couple of men here, Doc," Loder said, "just in case. Bring the others out to the mesa, pronto."

He turned and was gone, striding purposefully toward his lathered horse.

Riding south, Loder remembered an old Indian trail that angled off toward the low-lying lands. By following it, he could shorten the distance to the river crossing by ten or more miles. He rode Satan hard, and was within sight of Old Baldy—a familiar landmark in the shape of a smooth-topped mountain—before the rising sun tinged the dark crags with crimson and gold. Down below he could see the bunched herd, a dark mass in the glimmer of dawn light. The words of a song voiced by one of the Brazos-W night riders reached his ears faintly on the freshening breeze as he rode into the dip.

Most of the Brazos-W punchers were still in their blankets, or lying half awake, smoking. A few lounged near the chuck wagon, warming their hands at the crackling fire and sipping coffee. At Loder's approach, all heads turned, and hands dropped gunwards. A tall, grey-haired man stepped from the firelight with hand uplifted.

"Hold it, stranger," he ordered. "That's far enough. You lookin' for somebody?"

Firelight reflected on Loder's badge. Somebody voiced a profane remark.

"A Gawd-damned lawman, by cracky!"

"What the hell does he want?"

180

"All star-toters is pizen."

Loder ignored the comments.

"You rodding this outfit?" he asked the grey-haired man.

"I'm Lafe Naseby, foreman for Culp McQueen," the man said. "Who are you? I can see you're wearin' a badge, but—"

"Loder, U.S. marshal. There ain't time for a lot of talk, Naseby. *El Diablo* and his renegade bunch are likely to throw down on you at any time. There's thirty or more of the buzzards headed this way right now to smoke you out and run off the herd."

Naseby stared. He swore.

"The hell you say!" he exclaimed. "*El Diablo*! I sabe that dirty sidewinder. Stole a thousand head off Ben Stern just a month ago. We was told to expect trouble near the border. Y'hear that, boys? *El Diablo* and his greasers are plannin' to wipe us out. Wal, by Gawd, if there's to be any drygulchin', I reckon we'll beat them varmints to it. Much obliged, Marshal. Curly, you and Slim roust out the boys and tell 'em what's afoot. Take some of 'em and stake out near them rocks. Me and the rest of the crew will hole up in the brush around the bend yonder. It won't matter if the herd does start to run wild now. They'll only head for the river and save us the trouble of shovin' the critturs across. Move it, you hombres. You takin' a hand, Marshal?''

"I reckon. I want *El Diablo*. There's a bunch of vigilantes riding out from town should hit that crew about the same time they figure to hit the herd.''

"It's about time somebody did somethin' about that damned renegade,'' Naseby complained. "Say, are you the same Loder who used to ride for the Rangers? Reed Loder? I heard you'd turned gunslinger.''

"Can't always believe what you hear, Naseby. Better hurry. We don't have much time.''

The foreman nodded. He issued swift, concise orders. Bleary-eyed punchers, shivering in the first grey light of dawn, hurriedly dragged on range clothing, belted guns and saddled their horses. Naseby, checking the action of the forty-four holstered low against his hip, swung to the saddle.

"Let's go,'' he said. "We'll give them curly wolves a taste of hell.''

With Reed Loder riding beside him, Naseby led the grim-faced, complaining Brazos-W riders toward the brush. The men with Curly and Slim split into groups, some crouching among the rocks, others taking cover behind trees and among the bushes. Two of the more enterprising stretched a lariat across the trail and secured it tightly to trees. They waited in the crisp, damp, early morning air. Light was spreading from the hills when the thunder of fast-moving hoofs

182

betrayed the approach of *El Diablo* and his raiders. Like ragged, merciless wolves, the silent band swung into the dip and rode fast for the brush-screened river. Had they reached the timber unseen, they would have been able to gun down most of the Brazos-W crew before the alarm was raised.

Instead, they rode around the bend into Naseby's trap. Tight-lipped, the foreman waited for Loder's signal. It came, two shots close together that lifted a grinning raider from the kak, flung his lifeless body into the undergrowth and emptied the saddle of the dappled grey racing alongside. Instantly gun-thunder reverberated. Powdersmoke fogged the trail. Horses reared and plunged, squealing in terror. Men screamed and died. Saddles emptied. The milling raiders, taken completely by surprise, never had a chance. Twenty men were killed or wounded in that first murderous volley. Denton Molloy, miraculously unhit, wheeled his horse and jumped the animal into the thickets. The remaining raiders turned their animals and raced back along the trail, only to run into Doc Haggerty and Big John Faulkner with the vigilante posse.

When the gunsmoke cleared, only three of *El Diablo's* men remained alive. There were hot tempers and long memories among the vigilantes. Ropes were uncoiled, shaken out, nooses flipped over handy cottonwood limbs. Big John didn't try to intervene. When the posse rode back to town they left three limp shapes dangling, swinging gently in the wind. Rough justice, but thorough.

Meanwhile, Reed Loder saw Denton Molloy quit the fracas and vaulted astride Satan. Molloy had a good start, but his mount hadn't the same reserve of stamina and speed as the black stallion, and Loder quickly overtook the outlaw. For reasons of his own *El Diablo* headed for town, as yet unaware that he was being pursued. The town was quiet when the renegade rode in, the streets almost deserted. At Doc Haggerty's place, Ruth Faulkner lay on the bed, fully dressed, with her eyes open, thinking, and willing herself to get up. In her room above the saloon, Kate Molloy, too, lay on her bed, preoccupied with thoughts about Loder and her brother, convinced that Denton Molloy would handle the situation, and convinced, too, that Loder would agree to throw in with her and Denton rather than die a horrible, lingering death at the hands of *El Diablo's* border wolves.

She didn't give a damn for Burl Fadden, lying on a hard bunk in a cell across the street. Fadden was a fool, a broken reed, of no further use either to her or her brother. But Reed Loder—Kate sighed, got off the bed and moved to the window. She looked out. By now, she thought, the raid must be over. Soon *El*

*Diablo* would send Vincente and some of the others to take care of Haggerty and that other fool, Faulkner. Kate had sneered when she'd seen the vigilantes ride out, convinced that inside of an hour they would all be buzzard bait.

A lone rider appeared at the end of the street. Kate, recognizing her brother even at that distance, frowned. Why was he in Twin Rivers, alone? If he went after Haggerty and the marshal himself, it meant revealing his dual identity. Then the sight of another rider wrung an involuntary cry from her. Reed Loder! How had he escaped? Did her brother know that he was being followed? Denton Molloy dismounted outside the jail. Kate watched, confused and uncertain what to do, saw him shoot the padlock off the door, kick the door open and go inside. Shots rang out. A man staggered onto the boardwalk and pitched headlong. Another shot blasted.

Kate's brother emerged, gun in hand. Burl Fadden was with him. Abruptly, the outlaw leathered his pistol. Reed Loder, dismounting in the shadows, was as yet unnoticed by either Molloy or Fadden. They were halfway across the wide main drag when Loder stepped from behind his horse and stood with legs apart, feet astride, his right hand splayed above his gun butt. *El Diablo* and the crooked saloonkeeper saw him simultaneously. Both men stopped. Denton

185

Molloy's green eyes narrowed. He swore. Fadden gaped, mouth open, then moved quickly away from the renegade, turned and ran, ignoring the pain of his twisted ankle. Limping, scuttling like a giant crab, he disappeared into the side street flanking the saloon.

Loder let him go and watched Molloy. *El Diablo* turned slowly until he was facing the Texan. His face was like hewn granite, his expression strangely calm.

"Loder!" he rasped. "I should have known it was you who warned the Brazos-W outfit. You set up that ambush, you badge-totin' stringbean. I should have known better than to let that fool sister of mine talk me into giving you a chance to live. But you won't be doing any crowing, gunslammer. I run this town. I run this whole territory. Ain't nothing changed. Within a week I'll have fifty men riding for me. But you, Loder, you won't be around. You've had a good run, tinhorn. Now it's finished. I'm ending it, as of now."

His draw was sheer poetry of motion, made with the smoothness and incredible swiftness that had made his name feared and hated throughout the entire West prior to his supposed massacre by an Indian war party. He drew one gun only. Loder, beaten to the draw despite his own uncanny skill, slewed sideways desperately. Lead punched into his shoulder even as his own weapon bucked against his palm; it tore through flesh and muscle and ripped out of his back.

186

The bullet's savage impact threw him against the hitching-rail, and he fell, rolling aside quickly, instinctively, as *El Diablo* shot again.

His own first shot kicked up dirt at the outlaw's booted feet. Then he was kneeling, and his thumb was lifting from the hammer spur a second time. Denton Molloy's second shot smashed Loder's leg below the knee. But in that same instant hot lead slapped dust from the outlaw's fancy vest, and *El Diablo* was staggering back, with blood staining the front of his buckskin coat and the vest and shirt underneath, forming a large, spreading patch. Surprise mingled with fear widened his eyes. He raised his gun, tried to steady his hand. Blood trickled from the corner of his twisted mouth.

"Damn you!" he muttered. A fraction of a second before his six-gun roared, a third slug from Loder's gun smashed into his heart. The tall renegade teetered. His eyes, already glassy, stared fixedly at the Texan. From across the street a piercing scream rang out. But all eyes were focused on Denton Molley, alias *El Diablo*. Slowly, like a felled tree, he pitched forward and lay face down in the dust.

Kate Molloy, watching, horrified, from the saloon window, screamed again. Savage fury mingled with grief and panic prompted her hasty departure. With her brother dead and Burl Fadden due to hang, there was nothing left for her in Twin Rivers. Now her only thought was to get away. But she would not, she resolved, go empty-handed. She snatched up the gunbelt looped over the bed-post, strapped the thirty-eight-calibre pistol round her trim waist, then opened the door and stalked along the corridor. The door of Fadden's upstairs office was ajar. Kate pushed it wide open, saw Fadden crouched in front of the big iron safe, stuffing papers and bills into a saddle-bag, together with small sacks of gold and silver coin.

So intent was he on rifling the safe that he didn't hear Kate enter until she was standing over him with the muzzle of her pistol only inches from his temple.

"Keep filling the bag, Burl," she told him coldly. "When you're all finished, I'll take it. Don't give me any trouble—partner."

The gun hammer clicked as she cocked it. Fadden gulped. Fear widened his eyes. But there was cunning, too.

"Kate!" he blurted. "What's the big idea? I didn't even know you were here. What in tarnation—?"

"You sneaking sidewinder! You were running out and taking every damn cent. Half that dinero is mine, you dirty skunk!"

"All right. You weren't here, leastways I didn't know you were. You'd have gotten your share later. Sure I'm pulling out. We're all washed up, Kate;

finished. I heard the shooting. Now that Loder's dead, I'm next on *El Diablo's* list. You can't fool me. I'm gettin' out while—"

"You're wrong, damn you! Denton's dead, not Loder. Lying there on the street with two bullet holes in him. Oh, we're finished all right. But you're not going anywhere, lover—not with that money."

Ignoring the threat of her gun, Fadden stood up. Kate should have shot him then. She didn't, and that was a bad mistake. Fadden faced her with the bulging saddle-bag dangling from his grasp.

"You cheap tramp!" he accused. "You were all set to ditch me for Loder and have that hellion brother of yours get me out of the way. I heard you talking to Loder just before I blew Jack Butane's backbone into his lousy guts. You—"

"Don't make me use this," Kate warned, raising her pistol. "Give me that saddle-bag and step aside. Force my hand, Burl, and I'll kill you. I won't—"

Suddenly Fadden swung the heavy saddle-bag, knocking her gun aside. It exploded, but the shot went wide. His fist lashed out and smashed Kate in the face, slamming her against the desk. As she fell, her head struck the corner of the open safe door. Blood spurted. She shrieked once, horribly, and was dead before Fadden grasped what had happened. Licking his lips, he backed away, gaping stupidly, then bent quickly and picked up the gun Kate had dropped, suddenly realizing what she had said about her brother being dead. That meant Reed Loder was out there on the street.

Fadden snarled like an animal. He jerked the curtains aside and stared out, and his lips writhed back from his clenched teeth when he saw Loder clinging to the hitching-rail with blood soaking his coat sleeve, and his left leg doubled under him. So, Fadden mused, *El Diablo* had crippled the long son. Grinning wolfishly, Fadden left the room and limped down the back stairs, out into the back alley. Kate's pinto was there, tied to a post. Fadden slapped the saddle-bag across the animal's withers, mounted and kneed the pony to a run.

As he rode out onto the main street, Doc Haggerty's posse and Big John Faulkner rounded the bend and thundered into town. A hoarse yell went up when Fadden was seen and recognized. Reed Loder, with one hand pressed against his shoulder wound, tried to reach the gun he had dropped. Fadden, yielding to panic and fury, shot twice at Loder under the pinto's neck. Both slugs burned close. Loder got the fallen six-gun and fired once. But nausea spoiled his aim, and the bullet merely ricocheted from the horn and tore through Fadden's cheek instead of his chest. He screamed, almost spilling from the saddle. Clinging to the slashed horn, he whirled the pinto and sent it racing toward the other end of the street. Faulkner's voice thundered in the keen morning air.

"Hold it, Fadden! Stop—or I'll shoot!"

Fadden kept riding, crouching low. Big John raised the rifle he was carrying, took aim and put a bullet through the fugitive's spine. The echoes from the shot were still resounding when Ruth Faulkner emerged from Doc Haggerty's front door in time to see her father kill Burl Fadden.

A knot of men gathered round the huddled corpse of *El Diablo*. Big John Faulkner dismounted stiffly. Doc Haggerty slid ponderously to the ground. Ruth was already pushing through the crowd toward Reed Loder. His face was twisted with pain, and he was supporting his full weight on his right arm, clinging to the rail again. His gun lay in the dust. He forced a grin, though his teeth were gritted together.

"Oh, Reed!" Ruth cried. She laid a hand on his sound arm. Loder staggered.

"I'm all right," he lied. "A mite tuckered out is all. We whipped 'em, Ruth. Whipped the whole damn bunch."

"Yes, Reed. You whipped them, you and Father and Doc. Thank God it's all over. I was wrong, I know that now—wrong about so many things. And I'm sorry. But you mustn't stand here. You're hurt! That shoulder! Your leg!"

"They ain't more'n scratches, honey."

He released the rail, reached for her and drew her close. He kissed her.

"I'll be patched up and ready to ride in time for supper," he told her. "Don't forget we've got a date. After that, I reckon I'll be returning this badge to Governor Kendrick. Then I'll be coming back, Ruth. I reckon—"

He was still grinning when they carried him across the street and into Doc Haggerty's parlor.

192